EVERGREEN VALLEY MURDER

A DAMIAN GREEN SERIES MYSTERY

ALEC PECHE

For my great friend and first reader, GM, thank you for all the input you've provided to this and all my books. Kudos for KP for your copyeditor skills. I couldn't do this without you.

Thank you to my hometown for putting on the best Independence Day parade that gave me the idea for this story.

CHAPTER 1

The roar of the crowd was audible to Hermione Knowles despite being under water. The pool wall was ahead. She had just made her final underwater flip before stroking for all she was worth on the final leg of the one-hundred-meter freestyle race at the California North Coast sectional swimming championships. A quick glance between swim strokes across the water indicated that no one was in front of her. It was time to dig deep and touch the wall first. She pulled each hand through the water, kicking ferociously forward. She saw the wall approaching. She was out of oxygen, her arms and legs dead from her final burst. She stretched as far as she could forward and touched the wall. Panting, she held onto the wall, pushed her goggles on top of her head, and strained to see the scoreboard and her name.

Her fellow racers had all arrived and were also holding onto the pool wall. Like her, they were trying to catch their breath while awaiting the final time verification. Then, the race results flashed in big red letters on the scoreboard, "Knowles."

Her name flashed in first place, she won the race for herself, her school, and her coach. She pounded her fist in the water, and then fist-bumped her competitors, trying to show her sportsman-ship. She heaved her body out of the water, her heart still pounding with the effort of the race.

Hermione looked over to the stands where her guardians Ariana and Damian were standing and clapping for her. She grinned at them, and her first-place finish, throwing her arms in the air. This was the last race, and the school year ended in three weeks. She was excited to start her summer adventure working at Damian's firm.

School was great fun, and she was successful, but given the secrets about her parents, she could never fully let her guard down with her school mates. That added stress to her teenage years. She made her way over to the grandstands as soon as she could to hug her guardians.

"That was awesome, Kiddo!" Damian said.

Ariana stood with her arm around the teenager.

"Were you able to film the race?" Hermione asked. Her parents were in a witness protection program. Damian had been able to establish a permanent connection to them so they could stay in contact with their daughter and her life. They probably wouldn't be able to re-enter her life until she was off to college or beyond.

"I got the perfect film of your win. It starts with you stepping up onto the platform to make your dive into the pool and ends with your name flashing up in first place. Your parents will be very pleased with the race."

"Yeah! I want to stay and watch Meghan's race, and then we can leave. I'm going to the locker room to shower the chlorine off of me, so save me a seat."

They smiled as she hurried off to change out of her swim gear.

"I think Meghan's race is in about twenty minutes, and then we'll stop somewhere and grab a bite to eat. I know she's always hungry after she swims," Damian said, glancing at his watch.

Twenty minutes later, the three of them were on their feet, cheering for Hermione's teammate. She was a year behind

Hermione in school and finished in second place. What an accomplishment for their high school and their coach.

It was a Saturday afternoon in May. They were about three hours from home in the middle of California in a city that hosted state swim finals every year. Clovis was a suburb of Fresno, and the temperature was already a dry eighty-four degrees. They would be glad to get out of the heat, sun, and pool reflection and into the air-conditioned car for the drive north. Ariana lived in Belvedere and Damian on Red Rock Island, both located in San Francisco Bay. Once they arrived at Damian's house, he would upload the video of Hermione's race and connect her to her parents. She could narrate the competition for them while communicating over a secure connection. The two ladies would spend the night on the island along with Miguel, Ariana's Portuguese water dog.

In the morning, Ariana and Damian planned to follow Hermione while she navigated the bay in Ariana's pontoon boat. The teenager was going to work for Damian and needed a way to reach his office in Richmond. She would be using Ariana's boat to do the twenty-minute commute between Belvedere and the Richmond marina. She'd taken a boat safety course and got her license. This was the final dry run on a busy weekend day out on the water to prove to her guardians that she would be safe at the helm by herself. Once she reached Richmond, Damian created a rideshare account for her to get a ride the remainder of the way. Of course, on some days, they could commute together.

It was a massive responsibility for the teenager to be alone on the well-traveled bay. She would have to be alert to avoid smaller boats as well as ferries. Large ships wouldn't be in her traffic path, but certainly, a ferry could destroy the pontoon boat and Hermione along with it. Like any teenager, she loved her cellphone, however, unlike every other kid, she'd grown up fast with the problematic life engineered by her parents.

They stopped at a fast-food restaurant close to the competition site and were at the marina in Richmond by late afternoon. Ten minutes later, they all visibly relaxed as they locked the boat down on Red Rock Island's dock, and entered Damian's house. Damian set up the connection and uploaded the video for Hermione's conversation with her parents. They left the teenager to talk to her parents.

Ariana and Damian were soon relaxing in Adirondack chairs with a glass of wine in hand. Miguel was all about playing fetch, while Damian's cats, Bailey and Bella sat nearby under a table looking upon the dog with disdain.

"It's so sad that Hermione's parents are missing out on the joys of raising her. They can only watch her progress from a distance," Ariana mused, then cringed as she thought of all Damian was missing as his wife and daughters were murdered by an escaped convict.

Damian replied, "I don't feel sorry for them. Their situation is entirely of their own making. I created the connection to Hermione for her sake, not theirs. It's amazing that such irresponsible parents could create such a wonderful teenager. Their loss is our gain."

"Yeah, I feel lucky to have her in my life. She's everything I could wish for if I had ever had my own child. I think that once she leaves us, she'll always remain in contact as she likes and respects us. Maybe we should move on to a happier conversation. What project are you going to have her and Jacob work on?"

Damian smiled at her change of topic and replied, "I spoke with my team about how we were going to navigate getting work done with the two teenagers in the house. They're going to be mentored by Haley and Chris so that we parents are not involved. I'm assigning them the development of a privacy application that people can download to alert them and offer the opportunity to block anything that is tracking them."

"Wow, that's no small task. Will Jacob and Hermione have time to complete the app by summer's end? Do they have the coding skills to do this?"

"When we decided on their assignment, we set about teaching them coding, so they've been studying it for the past month and doing well. Lily, our math wiz, and Jacob's mom designed the course. Haley and Chris had a plan of how they want to develop this application, so I think that they might succeed. If they don't finish, we may look at some evening or weekend hours in the fall to finish the project. If we don't finish by mid-fall, someone else will beat us to market."

"That sounds exciting. I'd love to drop in when they have a progress report or final product to see what they accomplished. You know me, I'm always looking for talent."

"Are you trying to steal my employees?" Damian asked, grinning.

"Yes, if they're future stars!"

Hermione walked out of the house and sat down in the third chair, taking over pitching balls for Miguel.

"Did you have a good conversation with your parents?"

Hermione paused before answering, thinking about her feelings, which were a jumbo.

"Mom was crying because she wasn't there in person, and Dad was proud of my first-place finish."

"But?" Ariana nudged.

"I found myself resentful that I never got to participate in all of this stuff because of the decisions they made. Maybe if I started practicing earlier, I might have gone to the Olympics. It's their fault that I'm not getting that chance."

"Maybe, you would have injuries from overuse by now too that would have prevented you from going. Besides, you took first place. What's the Olympic qualifying time for your race?" Damian asked, knowing that Hermione would have looked it up.

"I'm two seconds slower than that time. It doesn't sound like much, but I was completely gassed today. I couldn't move my arms as I got one stroke away from the wall. That could have stopped me from winning."

"If it is that important to you, we could hire a coach, and see if you're capable of shaving the two seconds. You won't get to the Olympics this year, but maybe you could compete at the World finals next year, and be in line for the 2024 games. You would be twenty at the time, not a terribly old age for a swimmer."

"Let me think about that. I guess the other question I should ask is that the sport I'm best at? Could I get there on a soccer team?"

"What do you know about Olympic goalkeepers?"

"I'm short by two inches, but maybe I haven't finished growing."

"So what do you want to do?" Ariana asked. "You know we'll help you in whatever way we can for whatever sport interests you."

"I know. I guess that's what has me so mad about my parents is that their pleasure in my win today was tempered by their concern about was I safe? It never crosses my mind to worry about my safety when I'm around you two. I just know, if we get into trouble, Damian will figure a way out of it."

"Kiddo, that's kind of you, but I don't have superpowers. I would advise any girl, not just you, to always watch your back. It's not just the people who are after your parents, it's that the world is full of crazy, unpredictable people. I won't always be on the scene to save you," Damian advised.

"I know that, but you've given me the confidence to believe in myself, and you guys to save me if that makes sense? I made it into my safe room at my parents' house, but they didn't. I didn't know if that was a one-off, or if I was good. Now I know I'm good."

Ariana smiled at the teenager, "Just remember that when any friend wants you to do something you don't want to do, that it's your turn to find that belief in yourself, and remove yourself from the situation. Like Damian said, we won't always be there to save you, but you've got a brain, and it's up to you to use it."

"Oh my gosh, now you sound like a parent. Sometimes I forget you are one."

Damian and Ariana just smiled at each other as Damian grabbed Ariana's hand and said, "Don't ever forget we're old adults and can bring on the parent routine at a moment's notice. Personally, I think we're doing a good job raising you, and I can't wait to see what the rest of your life has in store for you."

"That's really sweet, Damian. Thank you both, and if I forget to tell you often, I love living with you and being your teenager."

Damian reached for her, pulling her in for an awkward group hug with Ariana given their positions in the chairs, but it got the point across to the teenager that she was loved in return.

CHAPTER 2

After a peaceful night, Damian and Ariana followed behind Hermione as she navigated the Richmond marina and then across the bay to Ariana's home. They couldn't find anything that the teenager could do better in her navigation. Damian left the ladies and returned home to get some work done.

In the afternoon, he received a call from Natalie Severino, the retired detective that solved his family's murders eight years ago when she was on the force. Now she worked cold cases for the San Jose Police Department.

"Hey Natalie, what are calling me on a Sunday for? I thought you retired types only work Monday through Friday."

She chuckled and replied, "I just returned from a vacation and found an intriguing cold case to work on sitting in my inbox. So I called you on the off chance you would pick up my call on a Sunday."

"What's intriguing about it? That's not a word you use often."

"A woman was murdered during a Fourth of July parade fifteen years ago. I was a relatively new detective at the time, and I remember the mystery of the murder that we, unfortunately, never solved. There was a ton of people around, so you would have thought we would have a witness, but no, no one saw anything. I thought that maybe you could use your giant computer to reconstruct the parade through photos posted that might give us a clue."

"There was less posting of pictures fifteen years ago. Social media was just getting started in 2005, and there may not be a lot of photos available."

"True, but the parade has used the same photographer for the past twenty years or so. We can start with the one-thousand photos she and her amateur photographers take each year."

"Okay, what do you know of her murder? How did it happen?"

"At the time, the SJPD determined that she was shot at nearly the front of the parade with a paralyzing agent via a dart. As she was in costume as a prop, no one noticed she was dead until the end of the parade when she didn't climb down with the rest of the float riders."

"That had to be a shocking discovery. Wow."

"It was. Imagine someone in a cartoon character outfit falling over dead at your feet. The parade lasts about ninety minutes, and so rigor mortis hadn't set in yet. There were ambulances and first aid close by, and they got to her in under three minutes, but it was far too late at that point."

"Is the parade still going on?"

"Yes. In fact, this year marks forty or so years. I think most people forgot about the murder or were ghoulish enough to wonder what would have happened the following year of the parade. The murderer was one and done, though."

"That sounds personal unless there was a serial killer wandering the city at that time."

"That was our conclusion, but family and co-workers all had verifiable alibis. There were no other poison dart murders ever in the city, so if it was a serial killer, he or she moved onto another part of the world."

"It does sound like an intriguing case. Where are the family members now of the murdered woman?"

"I don't know. That's part of the work I'll do on my end. The case hasn't been worked for about five years, so I'll be going through the records and updating the information. I'll re-run the dart for any DNA match, but that will take weeks to get back since this is a cold case."

"So, where do I get access to the photographers' pictures?"

"The local photography club volunteers at the parade. Fortunately, even in 2005, most photography was digital. So the original detectives assigned to the case collected all of the club's photos. And I'll send the disc copies overnight to your office in Richmond."

"Okay. I'll also do a search for any pictures outside of the photography club posted on the parade. I'll also do a worldwide search on poison darts."

"Thanks, Damian. I could do those searches too, but I know you're better at that than I am, and you're more likely to get more stuff in a search than I am. Besides, my clunky home computer might still be thinking about doing the search tomorrow."

Damian chuckled, "I bet. Why use your Moped, when you can borrow my Ferrari?"

"Exactly! Talk to you soon."

Damian liked working these cold cases with Natalie. He felt satisfied with the closure of the case and in some instances, with criminals going to jail, or a little girl being reunited with her parents. He would feel good about solving the death of a woman volunteering to be entertainment in her local community's parade, only to die from her own generosity. Yep, he was excited about the work. He wrote a quick program to search for photographs and poison dart incidents, and let his computers go to work. He then returned to a more basic need.

Damian gathered his fishing equipment, and Bella and Bailey followed him to the cliff's edge to watch him catch their dinner. It was a ritual for the three of them. He'd talk to the cats about the day, while they listened with occasional efforts at grooming. They loved it when he brought a wiggling fish on the end of his pole out of the bay. They would take a few swats at the fish before he unhooked it and put in a pail where they could watch it swim around. It was the best time of the day for them.

With the cats' dinner caught, he returned inside to see what his computer was doing. It was a small search in the grand scheme of things, but photographs could be slow to sort through, so he expected the poison dart incident data. Besides, he didn't think there would be many incidents.

He was wrong. The number of incidents, both real and imagined, was huge. There were conspiracy stories of exotic weapons manufactured and used. There were articles written about Hollywood props used in James Bond movies, and Amazonian Jungle tribes used darts as poison agents for hunting. He sighed and thought, this is going to take a while to sort out. He didn't feel like sorting through that mess at the moment. The photography search was continuing, and so he left the cold case alone and focused on other projects.

His company had two successful product launches in the past year. He had high hopes of another successful start of the project he was going to assign Hermione and Jacob. He was increasingly concerned with the lack of privacy that mobile phone users experienced while using their phones. So many companies track movements around planet earth, and more recently inside retail stores. He approached the problem from several angles trying to decide how to solve it while considering the major phone manufacturers' operating systems. He also looked at what was already available on the market. He settled in his mind that the data sellers had become too big, rich, and powerful. So he was going to not only solve the problem for the consumer but do so in a manner that was very detrimental to the data companies. His plan was to scramble any data on location collected by Bluetooth beacons.

He saw his plan working in two phases; first, the mobile phone app would identify which applications were connecting with beacons. Some news apps and other non-retail apps tracked phone owners even when they weren't open. Damian's solution was simple, block all beacon signals from reaching the mobile phone. His team would create an app that users could download and shield their phones. He would charge ninety-cents for the app, and all earnings would go to the two kids for college funds. All the way around, an excellent plan for his company.

As the sun set over San Francisco Bay, he took a few moments to reflect on his life. Some would say he was living a good life. He had more money than he could spend in his lifetime, a beautiful house in a beautiful location, an awesome girlfriend, a wonderful teenager to raise, and an innovative company to lead. He didn't feel lucky, though, as his murdered wife and girls' souls floated over to him across the waves of the bay. He had this urge to look for their faces in the mix of fog, clouds, and sunset colors swirling around him. He took another sip of wine, and it all disappeared and his fanciful imagination along with it. The sun was below the horizon, and his angels had flown away.

CHAPTER 3

Ariana dropped Hermione off at school and then headed south to Silicon Valley. She advised several start-ups in a variety of fields, but most of them were biomedical. Her husband had died young of cancer, leaving her financially well-off with a desire to find a cure for illnesses like the cancer that took his life. Today she was heading to Viramic, her start-up that was working on a solution to viral infections. Viruses, cancers, and bacterial infections were like a game of whack-a-mole. As soon as a solution was found for one, another variation appeared. There was a family of viruses that were transmitted between animals and humans. Viramic had an idea on how to break the replication once it reached humans. She had been reading up on the science trying to keep up with the company. Still, she had no medical training, and beyond college biology, not much of a science backing. She was very excited about the company and had a different relationship with this start-up, than most of the companies she invested in. In most of her start-ups, she was a silent investor that read progress reports in the format of powerpoint. With Viramic, she found herself deeply involved. She's spent time in their labs understanding their research, and edited their application to the FDA. For whatever reason, she found herself taking a personal interest in the company.

Today she was reviewing a budget expansion. If she agreed, it would be the most money she ever put into a company, limiting her ability to fund expansions for her other start-ups for several years. She could have coordinated angel investors, but she felt it was imperative to keep Viramic's work a secret. She'd seen a few large pharmaceutical companies swoop in with staff and resources and beat a smaller company to the punch once they understood the concept they were chasing. She vowed not to let that happen to this company. She'd even thought of asking Damian to be an investor as she knew she could trust him, and he could create a cloak of secrecy around the company. She would make up her mind about that by day's end, depending on what she heard during the presentation.

An hour later, she arrived at the company's offices. Later that afternoon, as she was driving back home to pick up Hermione, she decided on her course of action. She used her mobile headset to call.

He answered on the first ring, "Hi, how's your day going?"

"Good. I have a proposal for you and wanted to invite you to dinner to discuss. It's rather lengthy and expensive, but I think you could help one of my companies that I'm an advisor and investor to."

"That sounds intriguing. I should be able to get to your dock by six. Does Hermione have any plans this evening?"

"She's heading into final exams, and all of her athletic pursuits are at an end at the moment. So unless she's planning to meet with friends after school, she'll be joining us."

"That's good. I can tell her about the project that she and Jacob will be working on. She's really good at keeping secrets, but I want to talk to her about keeping industrial secrets and confidentiality in the workplace. It never hurts to go over that more than once."

"Part of the discussion I want to have with you is about industrial secrets and espionage. I want to be able to prevent it in one of my companies, so it looks like we have intersecting interests tonight."

Ariana heard what sounded like a crash in the background, and Damian said, "Whoops, got to run, one of my projects just crashed."

Ariana smiled at her car's dashboard, where the call had just been disconnected. Damian had a variety of projects being worked on at any given time, and he welcomed failure as much as success as that would make his final product better.

She looked up and briefly admired the orange-colored steel of the Golden Gate Bridge as she passed under its iconic beauty. Rush-hour traffic meant she had more time to admire the view, but she had to keep an eye out for bad drivers. She continued north on the highway toward Hermione's school and pulled up with perfect timing as the teenager walked through the front gate of her school. They were off and arrived home in a few minutes.

"Damian will be over for a business meeting with me tonight, and he also wants to talk with you, so we're having dinner with him, okay?"

"That's cool. I've got some homework, and then I'll help you with dinner. What are you making?"

"I don't know," Ariana said with a smile. "I invited him before I took a look at what I had in the refrigerator. If all else fails, we'll get take-out, but first, I want to see what I have on hand."

"Okay, see you in a bit," and she turned and retreated to her bedroom.

Ariana took inventory of the refrigerator's supplies and decided she had time to make traditional comfort food. Using her pressure cooker, she would make a roast with potatoes and vegetables, a salad, and forgo any dessert that night. She had an excellent red wine to pair with the beef. With her preparations underway, she sat down and outlined her proposal. She couldn't believe she was thinking of asking for millions from Damian for Viramic, and she didn't have a formal proposal prepared. She got a sketch pad out and sketched out her thoughts – the potential for the company, the need for funding at this critical junction, why Damian and the start-up suited each other, etc. Soon she was pleased with what she laid out and took a moment to change from work clothes into jeans, checking on the progress of her meat and vegetables. She started on a salad, then began peeling and slicing potatoes.

Hermione returned to the kitchen, sniffing the air. "Smells good, what are you making?"

"It's comfort food."

"What's that?"

"Comfort food is something you eat for either family gatherings or when you're feeling bad. It's usually not the best combination of protein, carbohydrates, and fat, but it really tastes good."

"Are you unhappy about something?" Hermione asked, with worry in her voice.

"No, not at all. I'm just fattening Damian up with delicious food as I have a proposal for him that I want him to say yes to."

"Oh. I get it," Hermione said, and then after a pause added, "When has he ever said no to something you asked for?"

Ariana thought about it and said, "Never, but there's a first time for everything, and I shouldn't assume he'll say yes. I want him to invest in one of my companies. I want him to say yes, not as a favor to me, but because my 'ask' stands on its own merits."

"Okay," Hermione said, deciding she didn't always understand the adults in her life. "Do you need help?"

"Can you watch the potatoes and mash them when they're done cooking?"

"You bet. Mashed potatoes would be my comfort food."

Ariana just smiled at the teenager, and added, "Yeah, they're mine too."

She looked out the window to see Damian's speedy boat

pulling into her dock. He hopped out, carrying a laptop bag, bent down to take the ball from Miguel, and played a short game of fetch with the dog.

Ariana poured glasses of wine and proceeded outside with one for Damian. It was good to sit in the fresh air and watch him play with the dog. Hermione was inside, putting the finishing touches on the potatoes, and setting the table. Judging by his face, it had been a good day for all of them. When Miguel looked like he had enough exercise, she invited him inside to dine after getting fresh water for the dog.

Soon they were stuffed with Ariana's comfort meal. During dinner, they discussed where they wanted to travel that summer on vacation. There would be time to go somewhere just before she started back to school in the fall.

"So I need to talk with Hermione, and then you want to talk to me," Damian said to Ariana. "Who wants to go first?"

"I think my discussion might be longer than yours with Hermione, so why don't I clean up the kitchen while you two talk."

Damian and Hermione were talking in the living room. She could hear the gentle rumble of voices, and she joined them once she finished.

"Do you have things squared away?"

"I never doubted for a minute that Hermione would keep secrets, and understand the confidentiality of the project I'm going to have her work on, but we were discussing Jacob, and how she could influence him on the subject. He's an unknown for me, and I really hope I don't have any leaks there, but Hermione will keep her eyes and ears open."

"He's all yours now," Hermione said, standing up. "I've got a date to play Fortnite, so I'll see you in the morning."

"Have a good time and win," Ariana said as she waved the girl off.

"So on to your proposal. What do you need help with?"

"I was thinking in the ballpark of a fifteen million dollar investment and a cloak of secrecy," Ariana replied while walking over to the kitchen to grab her charts she put together.

"Go big or go home, huh?"

"Something like that," she said, and she went through the presentation and her thoughts about his involvement.

"What an intriguing company you have here, and I understand the race to a solution and the issues around corporate espionage. I'm interested in helping your company, but not in the order you want. I think the greatest risk is your science being stolen, so I'd like to put some security around the company before I invest in it. If I can't lock it down, then there's a good chance my investment will get flushed down the toilet."

Ariana thought over his words and had to agree.

"Unfortunately, I think you're right. I had thought about all the good we could do if we could expand the lab space, but that work might be gone in a blink of an eye if we can't hold on to the technology. What do you have in mind?"

"Your biggest risk is your own employees. I would up the security in your lab, on your computers, and I would do security searches on each employee daily. I assume they've all signed nondisclosure agreements?"

"Yes to the nondisclosure agreements. How soon could you put your security suggestions in place at the company?"

Damian thought about the details in her presentation, the supplies in his home lab, and the work that needed to be done at Viramic's headquarters based on how Ariana described the building.

"If I start on it now, I could have it done by the end of the week. I need some kind of legal authority to get involved with this whole project. Tell me about your organizational structure and articles of incorporation."

After more discussion, they came to an agreement on what was to be done and how. Damian thought about spending the night at her house, but he had a lot to do to protect her start-up company, which was more important.

He smiled to himself as he thought of how he went from basking in the sun two days ago, cheering Hermione on. Now, he was absolutely overburdened between the cold case from Natalie, and now the security issue for Ariana. The women in his life sure kept him busy.

CHAPTER 4

Damian worked hard over the next seventy-two hours, securing Viramic. He'd informed Natalie that he would be delayed working on her cold case. In the interim, she'd sent him an update of where the case and players were now including the sad information that the victim's husband had passed away two years ago from a heart attack. He might still be a suspect, but he was beyond justice now. At the time of the victim's death, he had a vague alibi. The detectives at the time had been unable to verify the alibi one way or the other. He said he was at home mowing the grass, and the neighbors remembered the sound of a lawnmower, but anyone could punch holes in that story. Other than that family update, there wasn't any new relevant information from Natalie.

Damian went back to the two computer searches he'd set up days ago. The photography reconstruction of the parade hadn't worked as there simply wasn't enough timestamps matched to the location of the photographer. Two photographers standing at two different locations could snap a photo at 10:30am and show different views. It would have to be put together manually, and he wasn't going to go that route until he had something more specific to look for.

He'd found curious information about the murders – more people had died on floats around the world in the five years around the time of her death. People were dying in a variety of methods, including electrocution, inhaling carbon monoxide, being run over by a float, or having something fall on a float rider. It was an astoundingly weird collection of deaths, but only Natalie's case was determined to be a murder. He sketched out the dates, locations, how people died, and some personal facts about each victim. It was rather stunning. He sent Natalie a copy of his diagram and was unsurprised when his phone rang a few minutes later.

"This is amazing, Damian. It's clear from the notes of all the detectives that have worked on this case that everyone looked for deaths related to poison darts. Still, I can't remember a single investigation into parade float deaths. There's a pattern here. Did the pattern stop seven years ago, or did you limit your search to a period ending seven years ago?"

"Good question. I limited my search to a specific time. I'm going to go back now and do a twenty-year search for the same topic, and we'll see if the deaths are continuing even today."

"Thanks, Damian, and wouldn't that be something if we have a serial murderer, who's been on the loose all this time killing innocent people trying to help their communities on parade floats?" Natalie said.

"I know when I mapped it out, I got a chill over what might be going on."

"Do you think your supercomputer might figure out where the murderer might strike next?"

"If only it were that easy, but I might be able to offer some predictions."

"I can't wait to see what you'll come up with."

Damian ended the call and wrote a new program to sift

through the data worldwide, as well as a probability of where the killer would strike next if he or she was still active. He'd never tried this kind of probability analysis before, and only after he looked at what the computer came up with would he know if he did it right.

He left his lower-level lab while his computer went to work. It was time to catch some more fresh fish for Bailey and Bella. He needed to review the plan that Haley and Chris had developed for the two teenagers to follow in developing the privacy app. They would be starting work in two weeks, but first, he had a coding training session that they could begin at any time. Their school-work took priority at this point, but the coding training was set up to be fun, and both kids had tried it likely as a break to studying for their final exams.

Damian returned to the lab to find his computer had finished, and indeed the parade float deaths were continuing. Some of these would absolutely be ruled as accidents because they were, and other deaths would be ruled as accidents because of an insufficient investigation into their deaths. The most recent death was just over two weeks ago in Mexico in a Cinco De Mayo parade in Puebla, Mexico. Whoever was their serial killer, he or she had the means to travel the world visiting the various parades. Several cities in the United States had large Cinco De Mayo parades that the killer could have attended and perhaps may have visited during the past decades, instead they had chosen the parade location where the actual battle of the Mexican army over the French army had taken place. He wondered if the killer only picked the original commemorative site, but then he thought of the cold case. This had been an Independence Day celebration in California, not in Bristol, Rhode Island, which had the oldest continuing Fourth of July celebration. The killer could have chosen Philadelphia, where the Continental Congress signed the Declaration of Independence. The more he dug into this case, the more interesting it was, and the more ways he found to look at the data of float deaths.

He also looked at the computer's projections for the next death. The top of the list was the Copenhagen Carnival at the end of the month, which would give them several weeks to prepare if true. However, there were other parades around the world, and the projection came with only a forty percent accuracy.

The deaths were so numerous that he didn't want to waste his time plotting them out like he did the initial data. Natalie would be better at deciding what was a real accident, and what was a murder made to look like an accident. The data did prove that the husband wasn't the killer as the float deaths continued after his death.

Parades were on land and water, in boats, on motorized floats, trailers, and horse-drawn carriages. Their killer had seemingly attacked them all. A float was a float. Damian thought about what could possibly set off someone to spend the next twenty years killing innocent people on floats? Most people that rode floats were volunteers for a charitable cause, not leaders whose decisions might anger a group of people. Besides, this killer had gone all over the world to find his or her victims.

Damian wrapped up all his thought as well as his data and sent it to Natalie. For the second time that day, she called him an hour later, excited by his latest data and observations.

"Really Damian, the SJPD needs to hire you as a consultant to set up an analytics section. You provide so much useful data that I feel sorry for the detectives still on the job that don't have you as a resource."

"That's a nice compliment, Natalie, but I'll pass on that opportunity. People need to believe that data can help them solve problems. If your old department hasn't set up a division called analytics by now, then they don't believe in it. Did you see the projection for the next parade that your killer may strike? Please note that it's one of the lowest levels of accuracy that I've seen in a while. This person has been very active over the last twenty years in disrupting parades. I was scratching my head earlier, trying to imagine what the precipitating event was that caused this killing spree to start, and I couldn't come up with anything. I'd be interested in hearing from your experts on what the motive might be as that would be new data I could enter into the system and perhaps do something with."

"I'm going to discuss this with my Lieutenant in the morning. I think we'll have to bring in the FBI and Interpol, given the scope of these deaths. Are you available to come to police headquarters tomorrow if I need to explain anything?"

"I don't know, Natalie. Ariana is having problems with one of her companies, and I'm helping with that, and she remains my first priority. I'm sure I could be available by phone to answer any questions or provide any explanations, but I'm not sure I can be there in person. Let me know what you need tomorrow after you've had a conversation with your Lieutenant."

"Okay, Damian, I'll do that. Thanks so much for your help with this. When we started working on this case, I really thought the photographs were the key to solving the case, but now after reading your explanation, I can see that was just wishful thinking. At least you've come up with a new and promising way to look at the case. Have a great night."

Damian had a feeling that the next day was going to be full of competing priorities. Best to get a good night's sleep so his brain would be in top gear the next day.

CHAPTER 5

Damian was woken from a sound sleep by an alarm, which he thought was an intruder on his island. Then he realized after looking at his phone, it was coming from somewhere else. He called Ariana.

"I see that someone is trying to break into Viramic. Should we call the police?" she asked.

"I don't think so as it's a cyber attack, not a physical attack, on your company. Besides, the technology I installed is working. They're not getting in. What I want to know is where it is coming from. That will give us a clue as to how close the enemy is."

"Sometimes, Damian, you're scary good."

"Actually, Ariana think of how good your company must be if someone is trying to break into its computers."

"True."

"Okay, after bouncing off a dozen sites, I can see the IP address has coordinates inside North Korea. Wow, you've attracted some nasty enemies. Let me search for more information on that address."

"So what should we do?"

"Go back to sleep. The company is safe at the moment, but I

would bet the next attack will be a physical one if I could guess what the bad guys are thinking."

"What kind of physical attack?" Ariana asked with concern in her voice.

"When all else fails, they could blow up your business."

"How?"

"Given that you're the only occupant in your building, I would throw a bunch of Molotov cocktails at it, or get some explosives, although I would be the first to admit that I don't know how hard it is to get explosives. Or they could send a mail bomb. You likely have sprinklers in your lab, so if they could start a fire, they could expect water to destroy the lab."

"Those are terrible scenarios. I'm going to wake up the lab's leadership and get them working on some solutions to those scenarios. You've got the company computers backed up off-site, so it's the lab cultures and equipment that are vulnerable, in addition to the employees."

"Yes, so stop all deliveries coming to the building and hire a private patrol to guard it. Where possible, go buy the stuff you need in-person and bring it back. Let no one into the building and perhaps board up the facility, so nothing can go through its windows. You might choose to relocate to a new location that gives your building better protection while having the pretense that your business is located in its present location. Depending on how serious these bad guys are, you may add a protection detail to whatever scientists are critical to your company."

"You have any suggestions on where to move the lab? Is there another island like yours in San Francisco Bay?"

"Not that I know of, and my lab is too small to hold your company's research work. You might try NASA Ames Research Center at Moffett Field. They have a high-security campus. The other thing you might do is check with another Biotech firm to see if they have lab bench space. I don't really know the biotech space situation well in the Bay Area."

"Okay, let me call my people. It's a rude hour to wake people up, but then the alarm should have awakened them already."

"Keep me posted, oh, and the name of the company at the IP address that tried to break into your system is called Naegohyang. It's a state-owned conglomerate that produces clothing and, among other things – electronics."

"So that's probably where their hacking skill comes from – the electronics side of the company."

"Maybe, but North Korea seems to realize that they can do some of the greatest damage to the world without leaving their borders through hacking, and so they try. There's just no downside to being successful."

They ended the call, and Damian was fortunate to go back to sleep.

Ariana went to work, waking up the leadership of Viramic. Soon she had Julia Cortez and Stefan Weiss on a speaker call. The alarm had woken them up, but they were hesitant to call Ariana in the middle of the night as she was an investor not an employee. Still they were pleased when she called them. Julia was the lead scientist, and Stefan was her husband and Viramic's CEO. The couple was the biggest reason she had invested in the company. When she was pitched to as an angel investor, she looked for honesty and integrity of the leadership. No matter how great the product, if the presentation included any grand delusions, she was turned off.

"I heard the alarm go off, and Julia and I were discussing the threat, and we thought about to calling you, but decided you needed your sleep," Stefan said.

"I just got off the phone with Damian Green, and he said the threat came from a company called Naegohyang in North Korea. So I guess the good news is the work you're doing is so awesome that it has caught the attention of North Korea, and Damian's system alerted us and blocked them. The bad news is your research has the attention of that country."

"Yes, that was our assessment too. We must be on the right track to attract someone else's attention. Did Mr. Green have any suggestions on what to do next?" Julia asked.

"He had several, starting with you two. I think we need to get personal security for you. Julia, if you were killed, not only would it be a tragedy, but the company would fail. I'm going to find physical security for you, and the company today. Damian suggested that someone could throw a firebomb through the windows to try and destroy your research, by turning on the sprinkler system, and from fire damage. He suggested we board up the windows with plywood, stop all deliveries, and look for more secure lab space. He suggested the campus of NASA Ames Research as they have some high tech buildings. Stefan, do you have any ideas where Viramic might find high-security lab bench space in this region?"

"That's a good suggestion. There are other secure locations that I'm aware of, so I'll start making calls. I may have a contact at Ames. What about our other staff, do they need security as well?"

"That depends. You should write down the names of all of your employees and ask yourselves if they die today, will that end the company's work or merely inconvenience it for a while. I know that sounds heartless, but you're a start-up, and we're about to spend a fortune on security. Once you have your list ready, let me know how many employees are on that list for when I contact the security company. I don't mean to sound so ruthless in putting a value on some people's lives and not others. Still, you're a young company, and we want the majority of expenses to go for vaccine research and not for people security."

"We get it, and if you don't mind listening in at 3:30 in the morning, you can hear our discussion," Stefan said.

"Go ahead," Ariana said, and then listened as they ran down the twelve employees of Viramic and whether they would be missed if they quit their jobs in the next hour. In the end, they had a total of two employees beyond Stefan and Julia that needed security.

"Okay, I'll make contact with a security firm and hopefully get someone on the job today. If I can't get security personnel started today, I'd like to move you into hotels for now unless you have sophisticated home alarm systems. I've never hired private security before, so I don't know how soon they can start. Frankly, I'm paranoid enough that I'll want Damian to research the firm and protective detail that I settle on."

"Ariana, can we just say how much we appreciate your work and leadership for our company? You're going way beyond what the average company would expect of an investor," Julia said. "You're not just thinking about our product and our expansion, you're thinking about our survival on more than a business level. Your friend, Damian, is an asset that's been invaluable. If it weren't for him, we might have lost our company an hour ago."

"He is an amazing friend. Someday I'll tell you how we met. It will make you laugh and doubt my intelligence. So back to the company. You've finished testing on mice for the virus inhibitor, and you were planning to file with the FDA to report Phase I human trials. Once that application is approved, everyone will be after this company as the proverbial cat will be out of the bag. We should have discussed this last week during your presentation. Still, even I, as your primary investor, didn't realize the value of your research. We should have thought of beefing up your security. Oh well, at least we had something in place to save your research."

"We will check on the application tomorrow. Normally, it would take about seven years for our solution to be approved. Still, there's interest in fast-tracking some pharmaceuticals, and ours is one of them. I would expect to hear back within a month, and then some back and forth with the FDA, and I would guess we'll be able to begin manufacturing our product within three months. So, I'm going to look for space with that in mind. We'll outsource the actual phase II clinical trial. Still, I want us to do the manufacturing. So I look for new space today not just with our security in mind, but also the future manufacturing process," Stefan said.

"I remember that manufacturing need from your presentation. It seemed like at the time that was a way off, but looking at the big picture here, I agree that while looking for more secure space, you'll also incorporate manufacturing space," Ariana sighed, thinking of the mounting expenses. "I'll transfer financing into your account today. This really accelerates our spend rate."

"Yes, it does, and I'm open to other solutions, but I don't think it makes sense to move the company this week, and then again in say two months. Moving to a bigger, more capable space today strengthens our application with the FDA. At least we won't have the cost of labor for manufacturing immediately."

Ariana looked at the time and saw it was approaching four. She wouldn't get back to sleep, it was time to go to work on the security and financing for Viramic. Then she would have to figure out how to finance all of these new and unexpected expenses. She spent the next few hours examining her options before she had to drop Hermione off at school. It was likely going to be a long day, so she made arrangements for the teenager to be picked up from school, so she wouldn't have to race home. Her favorite start-up needed an extra pair of helping hands, and she determined that would be her today.

She was dragging when she returned home by eight that night. Hermione ordered take-out and had left Ariana's meal to be reheated. She soon had it warming in the microwave and poured a glass of wine. Hermione entered the kitchen when she heard Ariana arrive home.

"How was school today?"

"It's rather boring at this time of year. We're all just waiting for final exams, and there are no sports going on. You look very tired. Are you worried about the North Koreans?"

Ariana had explained about the attempted break-in on the way to school, and why she would be late getting home.

"I am worried about theft of the technology my company has created. I'm also worried about keeping the staff safe. We all really hustled today and found new space and security. The staff will be in a hotel for a week while we work out the details, but they have more protection, and no one knows where they're staying."

"How long will they have to worry about their technology being stolen?"

"I'm not sure. I think once the company has a patent and begins Phase II clinical trials, the danger will pass. So perhaps in no more than two months, the danger will be greatly diminished."

"What's a patent?"

"When you create something that no one else has done before you, then you file for a patent. Damian owns a bunch of patents for things he invented. It means that no one else can use his invention without his permission, as it is his intellectual property. So after we get the patent, the technology is recognized as ours, and if another country steals it, they have to pay us for patent infringement. That is unless you're North Korea or a few other countries. America doesn't have a patent treaty with North Korea, so they can steal all they want without penalty. Other countries also steal patents, so for those with the original patent, it pays to go into producing your product as soon as possible."

Hermione listened to the explanation and then said, "It's like cheating in school when you copy someone else's answer. You didn't have the answers yourself, so you stole someone else's work."

Ariana nodded, and added, "Yes and not only do you steal the answers for one exam, but you continue to steal them and get an 'A' at the end of the class, and you sold your stolen answers to other students for profit."

"That's not the right thing to do. You and Damian need to take these cheaters down."

"Damian installed systems to detect computer intruders, but it's up to the staff and me at Viramic to keep the company safe."

Hermione flexed her bicep then held out her fist for a bump. Likewise, Ariana returned the gesture, and then they both laughed and hugged.

Then Hermione had another thought, "What about you personally? Is your name associated with the company?"

"Nope. I'm a silent investor. Someone would have to hack into the bank account to find a wire transfer from me, then they would have to track back through Delaware and then the Cayman Islands to find my husband's name on the company. So I think I'm protected from detection."

"Good. It will be nice to have a quiet summer," Hermione said as she left to study for finals.

Famous last words.

CHAPTER 6

Hermione got her wish for a quiet end to the school year. She did well, maintaining her honor student status. After a weekend of relaxation, she was excited to report to work at Damian's company. She had driven Ariana's boat to his dock on Red Rock Island on Sunday night, and the two of them commuted on the pontoon boat to the Richmond marina where Damian's truck was parked.

"I'm so excited to start work today," Hermione said, seated in the truck.

"I know, Kiddo. I've got sunglasses on because you're beaming so much energy to the world. You're a private solar disc today."

She just grinned at him.

"Heck, we're going to make you complete forms for the first couple of hours. You know there's a lot of boring and tedious work and failure in front of you over the next few weeks. If it was easy, someone would have already done it."

"I know, but Jacob and I will succeed, and then we'll file for patents in our names, and we can use that on our college applications, and people will love our app."

"Individual humans will love your app, advertising companies and tracking apps will hate you. Be prepared for some shade thrown your way as I think you kids say."

She rolled her eyes at him and said, "Yes, shade is the word."

They arrived at Damian's warehouse. The ground level was mostly devoted to Pete's restaurant, a second location to his original in Oakland. A set of double doors with only a street address marked the entrance to Damian's company. He pulled out a key fob to allow them to enter the doors. Inside was a choice of a freight elevator or set of stairs. They chose the stairs, and again Damian used the key fob at the top of the stairs to enter his offices.

Hermione was delighted by the balloons and breakfast buffet that awaited her and Jacob's first day on the job. She and Damian were the last to arrive, and she fist-bumped everyone assembled. Having been to Damian's warehouse in the past, she knew everyone. She stood next to Jacob while Damian made a little speech.

"These two teenagers represent several new opportunities for the company. If we like the work they do, then they and maybe more teenagers will be back next summer. We can help kids take an interest in science and engineering by working here. Chris and Haley will be their supervisors, and no one is to cut them any slack. Yes, Hermione is my favorite teenager, and I'm sure that Jacob is Lily's favorite. Still, when she's here, I have high expectations of her. My hope is by the end of the summer, the four of you will have your names on a patent and a commercially available app that will help the average phone user protect their privacy. So welcome Hermione and Jacob."

The two teens socialized with everyone and ate. Then as promised, Damian had them complete employment paperwork. Once they finished, Haley and Chris took them to the ample open laboratory space and set them to work at a lab bench. Both of them had completed the tutorial on app design and were anxious to start. Hermione was older with an extra year of high school math, but Jacob was Lily's child, and she'd made darn sure he was good in math. Better still, each teenager favored a different smart-phone operating system, which was also suitable for the app design.

The teenagers went to Pete's restaurant for lunch, and to get to know each other better out of the range of the adults. Damian had Pete keep a weekly total of meals that his employees consumed, and he covered their bills.

"Is this not dope?" Jacob said once they put their order in.

"It is, but pretty much everything that Damian does is dope. We're living a dream here compared to our classmates. We get paid, we have cool people to work with, we get fed as much as we want. What could be better?"

"I wish one of my classmates was here with us," Jacob said after he took a sip of his drink.

"We're an experiment. If we do a good job, then Damian will hire teenagers every summer. I think he thought that since he knew both of us personally, he should start with us. I asked him last fall if I could work at his company, and he made it happen."

"So why did he add me?"

"I can't remember if Ariana suggested it or if he thought of you as another employee's kid. Regardless, I know he spoke with your mom before he made the offer to you."

"You call your mom Ariana? That's weird."

Hermione had always felt confused about what to call Ariana. She had her last name and was under her parental control, and she acted like a mom, but her real parents were out there and alive, though she likely wouldn't be reunited with them before she was an adult. Maybe she would talk to Ariana about it when she got home.

"We're in a work setting, so it seems better to call her by her given name. Anyway, she studied the child labor laws and deter-mined what the company needed to do to employ both of us. Why do you want your friend to work here, besides all the great food?"

"He's a genius at coding, and with his help, we would be done in a week."

"Really? We're both smart, and yet we need time to write all kinds of code and to do so for two operating systems. What makes him so fast?"

"He's been writing code for a couple of years, and even has a free app available in the store. His parents don't understand what he does, so other than our science teacher Mrs. Rios, he has no support."

"Did you tell your mom about him?"

"No, I wanted to see how this gig was going to go. I didn't want to try bringing Jordan here if I didn't like it myself."

"Maybe you won't like it. Everyone's been really nice on our first day, but we haven't mouthed off or failed at something yet."

"Really? You would say that? Can't you tell that failure is okay with this group? I love watching that short video of Haley crashing the drone into all kinds of things. That was a big failure, and yet all they did was record it and laugh at it. We'll be allowed to fail as long as we try."

Hermione already knew that about Damian, but she had wanted to see what Jacob thought about the company.

"So why don't you go talk to Damian sometime today, and get your friend hired. He's old enough, right?"

"Yeah, he just turned sixteen. He gets paid to tutor kids. Should I ask my mom first?"

"She would be on your side if she knows him and thinks highly of him, but it's Damian's decision to make, so I don't know what to tell you," Hermione said, in a rare moment of indecisiveness.

"Maybe I'll show him the app, and see if he'll interview him."

"Okay. Meanwhile, we need to plan our market research as that's our next step, according to Haley and Chris. They gave us this tracker so we can walk through retail stores, and see how they track us. I think we should walk all of the aisles of about eight to ten stores, big and small, that sell a variety of products. I think we should go together, so we can take notes, and agree on what we see, and how our respective phones respond. Do you agree?"

Jacob thought about her plan and nodded his agreement, "I admit I'm curious to see our results as until I heard what our assignment was going to be, I didn't know we were being tracked so much everywhere."

"Great, let's plan our journey for tomorrow. Damian arranged for a ride-share account for us to use, so we'll just get a ride to all of these places. I think we can do much of our research locally, but perhaps we should go over to San Francisco and hit Union Square or a shopping mall to see if we get the same data."

"I think we should go to San Francisco to verify our data. I would add that we should go to some small town, but probably the stores there can't afford to buy the beacon technology, and they probably know their customers and can track them personally."

The teenagers finished their meal, returned upstairs to their lab workstation, confirming their plan with Haley, and then mapped their research for the next three days. This was going to be fun, imagine being paid to go visit all of these stores, the two teenagers thought?

CHAPTER 7

The two North Koreans were in a small conference room in Pyongyang. Lee Nak-yon had promised to put his best hacker on the job to break into the American company. That hacker had failed, and General Thae Yong-ho was unhappy with him and his results. Kim Jong-un, better known as the Marshal to his people, the Supreme Leader of the People's Republic of North Korea would also be unhappy. Lee had spoken with the hacker who marveled at the security in the small company. Not only had his hacker been surprised he couldn't get in, but he was reasonably sure he'd been detected. Lee didn't care about being identified, as there were no consequences to his country trying. However, he was concerned that he hadn't been successful. Speaking the Korean dialect of the North, they discussed the failure of the assignment.

"I thought this man was your best hacker? What happened?"

"He is our best hacker. In fact, he entered the company last month and left a worm behind so he would have ease of access. At that time, he verified that they were very close to a solution to the virus."

"So what happened? Why did he fail?"

"He said that the worm was gone, and with each attempt to access the site, he had to stop and defend against a worm being put on his own system," Lee said.

"This is not acceptable. We need another solution for that company. Why don't we just destroy it? It's too close to a solution to the virus we intend to unleash on the world. We've been planning this for over two years. We cannot fail when we're this close to the release of our weapon."

"General, if we destroy the company, we slow them down a few months as they build their laboratory elsewhere. I think we need to eliminate the employees of the company so they can't rebuild. There are twelve of them, but our intelligence says that we only need to eliminate half of them."

The General studied a picture on the opposite wall of a local hotel, triangular in shape, while he contemplated what to do. He'd been successful in other countries with poisoning enemies of the state, but he'd never tried to eliminate six people in one location in a foreign country. When he was successful with this task, it would raise his standing in the party, and he wouldn't think about failure.

He nodded to Lee Nak-yon and said, "Let's develop a plan to eliminate the scientists. Do we have assets on the ground? Where is this company?"

"It is close to San Francisco. I don't know what assets we have close to the company. I only have a hacker trying to get into the company," Lee said, cringing that the General wouldn't like his response.

The General turned his attention on Lee and focused, deciding if Lee was disrespectful with his answer. He thought about terrorizing the man but decided that wouldn't gain him anything.

"Well, have your hacker keep trying to get into the computer systems at Viramic. I'll figure out how to physically attack the company. I'd like to listen in to the company's communications and find out how close they are to virus solution and their ongoing plans. I need to stay two steps ahead of this company in order to take it down. The Marshal has plans for world domination with this virus we're concocting, and we don't want some small company in our enemy of the United States blocking that domination."

"Yes, General. I will do that. We will try very hard to listen in on this company. Do we have a timeline?"

"In approximately one month, we will have agents spread out across the world carrying a virus guaranteed to devastate the economies of our enemies. Many people will be sick, and many will die. They will run out of equipment as they tried to save their people. It will make people afraid to go out to work, to school, even to get groceries. We will decimate businesses around the world. Tourism will stop, and the Western world won't know what to do with all the dead bodies that accumulate."

"You paint a terrifying picture, and I can see what a great position our homeland will be in if we succeed," Lee said, and then thought of something else. "Do we have an antidote to this virus here in North Korea?"

"We do not, but then we will make sure it doesn't spread here. Our borders are closed so we can make sure that infected people stay out. The people we've lined up to spread the virus around the world will leave our borders and travel through China to reach the remainder of the world. They will be given multiple vials of the infection to break open when they are in crowded spaces or on airlines. We hope that the virus will spread aboard airplanes, and then when they land, those people will go out and infect their own communities. It's a brilliant plan that our Marshal devised and directed."

Lee Nak-yon thought that he had seen all the tricks that his government played on the rest of the world. He was trapped in North Korea as he had a large family, and his escape would put their lives in danger. So, he, like millions of other North Koreans, did the bidding of the Marshal's regime. However, unleashing such a horrible illness on the entire world was terrifying. He had some family in South Korea, and others had left for China, Japan, and Mongolia, but he had no idea if any of them had made it out alive. Right this moment, they might be in work camps in the north being tortured, starved, and overworked. He would continue to do what the general needed and wanted, but he promised himself he would put some of his considerable brain-power to use, figuring out how to escape this awful country. He ran a successful business as much as anyone could operate a company under the state supervision of North Korea, but enough was enough. It was time to figure out how to get himself and family members he cared about out of this regime.

"General, is there anything else you need me to do? I have my best hackers working on the company in the United States. When they break through, they'll destroy all of the company's data, and while my hackers are there, they will try to locate and destroy any backups of the data. We do that by inserting a computer virus that will activate once someone tries to use the backup."

"That is more than I understand about how computers work. I just want to know that you succeeded," the General said, turning to leave, and then he thought of something. "Can you have your people do a background check on the employees of this company. I want a list of which employees might be open to a bribe as they are in bad financial circumstances, and the names of the employees that are critical to this invention they're creating to counter our virus."

"Yes, Sir. I will get you that list."

CHAPTER 8

Natalie was waiting for her appointment with the Lieutenant, who supervised her work on cold cases. She was so excited to share the data that Damian had found for this case. She thought back to her twenty years as a police detective and couldn't remember when she had such intriguing analytics for a case. She was excited to see where the department would take the case as it had national and international implications. She'd be the first to admit she would love to be sent to Copenhagen to search for the killer at their upcoming carnival.

She heard the door open and looked up, exchanging greetings with a detective with whom she used to work. The Lieutenant invited her into his office, and his door was closed once again with her inside.

"So Severino, tell me what you have. You said you had an update on our float victim from a decade ago."

"Yes, I do, Sir. This is turning into a compelling case. Let me tell you about my findings so far. When you assigned the case, I went back and updated the department's information about the individuals involved originally. I also did a search to see if anyone else had been killed with a poison dart. I thought I was going to be able to reconstruct the parade by having a computer arrange all the photos that were taken. We can identify who was in each frame, and who knows where that would lead. However, that didn't work. A number of photographers both assigned to the parade and families observing the parade took a lot of photos. Even though many of them are time stamped, the time stamping doesn't work. It depends on where the photographer was standing on the parade route as to what they saw at a certain time of day. Do you follow me?"

He nodded his agreement with her explanation and waved her to proceed with her report.

"As you know, in many of my cold cases, I use the computer expertise of Damian Green. He did a search on murderers who used poison darts as their weapon, and he came up empty, much as I had. Then he did a search of parade float deaths, and he struck gold. I'll just jump to the punch line and say, based on the data the computer found, there's a serial killer at work killing people on parade floats. It's going on all over the world and has been for at least the past fifteen years. I asked him to do a further analysis of where the killer might strike next, and his computer concluded that the next murder will occur at the Copenhagen Carnival next week."

Natalie waited for the Lieutenant's response. He was fast on his feet, and that's why he was a Lieutenant. Still, it sounded so far-fetched she expected pushback.

The Lieutenant had listened to Natalie Severino's explanation about the cold case. Her story was very hard to believe, but this expert computer friend of hers had pulled off some miracle solutions in other cold cases. He probably would've laughed at any other detective that provided the explanation she had just now. However, all he had to do was remember the lost child she and Damian had located on a prior case, and he knew she was on to something.

"Wow, that's a hell of a big picture to get my arms around. You're telling me there is a current serial killer that targets people riding on parade floats, correct?"

"Yes, sir."

"I assume you have a list of events you believe our killer to be connected to?"

"Yes, I do. I will admit that perhaps a few are real accidents, but otherwise, all of the deaths are the handiwork of one person."

"Well, this is a cold case, but now you have urgency because of a computer prediction of when and where the killer will strike next?"

"Yes sir, although Damian says it's one of the lowest probabilities his computer has ever come up with," Natalie said, looking through the paperwork. "He says there is a forty-percent probability that he is correct. He said that was rather low, but this killer's last victim was likely in a Cinco de Mayo parade in Mexico three weeks ago. There are many parades all over the world, and so that is what makes the projection hard to do."

"Is there any evidence that he strikes the same parade twice? He's been killing for a long time. You would think he'd run out of parades."

"Many countries have parades throughout their cities celebrating the same occasion similar to our Independence Day parades. There might be thousands of those in the United States."

"True," the Lieutenant mused. He was dumbfounded at the data that Natalie was presenting him. Usually, a decisive man, he needed to focus his brain and decide where to go next. He thought about the resources available to him at the moment.

"I'm going to pull in some additional detectives. I'd like to delve deeper into some of these reported deaths. I'd like you to take over the conference room, and verify the circumstances around ten to fifteen of these deaths today. We can't ignore the low probability of a potential murder by next week, even if it is far outside of our jurisdiction. So let's verify the data, and then we'll run it up the flagpole. Beyond the department's command, we will need to notify the FBI, and potentially the Copenhagen police, and perhaps Interpol. I think this might be the biggest Pandora's box I've ever handled in my career, but first, let's verify our data."

"Yes, Sir," Natalie said, excited about being on the case of such a huge monster. "I'll set up in the conference room, and start reviewing some of these deaths. Are you going to give the detectives an overview of the case, or should I?"

"Normally, I would have you do it, but I have a feeling I'm going to be giving this explanation to multiple people over the coming days, and I ought to practice on getting it right. If I can't convince my own detectives that this is a good use of their time, then it's not going to go well when I explain it to the higher-ups."

"Good point and I'll leave you to it."

Natalie left the Lieutenant's office and headed to the conference room. She spread her papers out on the table and plugged her laptop in. She took a moment to send Damian an email with the Lieutenant's plans. She smiled when he returned a thumbs-up emoji. She was splitting out the fifteen cases they would verify, targeting those that occurred in the United States.

She looked up when three detectives entered the room. Two of them she had worked with before her retirement. The third detective she vaguely recalled seeing in uniform. He must've passed the detective's exam. Natalie couldn't decide whether their expressions reflected disbelief in the data or awe in the case's breathtaking scope.

"Detectives, while I have a collection of float deaths during parades from around the world, I think we should focus on some of the cases that occurred in the United States. Our brethren in other police departments here are more likely to give us timely cooperation in verifying the circumstances of these deaths. Wouldn't you agree given that the Lieutenant wants us to verify fifteen cases today."

Detective Marcela Alvarez said, "I agree. Some of these cases have to be accidents or natural health events because people have heart attacks at random times. Does your data show a pattern? Does your killer strike once a month on the fourth Saturday or anything like that?"

"I haven't taken the time to calendar all the deaths on this list - there are over three-hundred, and not all of them are homicide. I don't think it would do for us to calendar the deaths until we know which are truly accidents or medical incidents versus suspected homicide. Also, some of these deaths occur in locations with poor detective resources, and there may not be enough information for us to determine the mode of death."

"Let's get to work. As a new detective, this case might be the most landmark case of my future career if someone's been killing that many people, in that many locations, over nearly twenty years," said Detective Chris Kiel.

The more seasoned and jaded detectives smiled benignly at the youngster then got to work. With laptops and cell phones at the four corners of the conference room, the room was abuzz as the detectives tried to verify the details of the parade float deaths. Nearly every conversation with a distant police department was filled with either disbelief or curiosity by the end of the call. Could a mass murderer have gotten away with all that was alleged in this string of cases?

Meanwhile, the Lieutenant had alerted his Deputy Chief about the case's potential. The deputy chief had warned the Chief, given the work underway, and the implications of the case. Gossip had spread through the division over the potential of the case, and everyone was eagerly awaiting news from the conference room. The tension grew over the day, culminating in a visit by the command officers as it was approaching the end of the day shift.

The Lieutenant knew that his three detectives, along with Natalie Severino, were discussing what they found in their phone calls to various police departments around the country. The Lieutenant had assigned Sergeant Alvarez as the lead detective in the case. Now he, the Deputy Chief, and the Chief were listening in as the four summarize their findings. They had concluded that twelve of the fifteen cases were suspicious.

"I hope you all can stay. I think we need to call the FBI immediately to get assistance with this case. Then someone will have to make contact with the Copenhagen police. I would like to control as much of this case as possible, but I can see this spinning out of our control. Natalie, is our Evergreen Valley parade victim the only case that occurred in our jurisdiction? I mean, we have many annual parades in this area. Our killer doesn't strike the same parade twice, but that's not to say there may be more than one murder in the same region for a different parade," Chief Gomez said.

"Just a moment, Sir," Natalie said, running down her printout looking for any other deaths nearby.

There was silence in the room while everyone awaited her answer.

"Sir, it looks like there is one more death in our area. We haven't researched this case to know more than it's a death. It occurred during a Christmas parade in Morgan Hill. That's not our jurisdiction, but it's close to Evergreen Valley."

"I have a lot more questions, but we need more resources to work on this case. I'm calling the FBI Agent in Charge in San Francisco, the Deputy Chief will contact the San Jose office, and Lieutenant if you would contact the Morgan Hill Police, let's plan on having a briefing in ninety minutes in the auditorium. Detectives, would you take some time to look at the data, and give us some broad analysis. I know you don't have details about each person on Natalie's roster, but based on your sampling, we know that perhaps eighty percent of the cases are suspicious. How many are inside the United States versus the rest of the world? What's the ratio of male and female victims? Young or old? You get my drift."

The Chief left to return to his office as everyone scurried to carry out his orders. Natalie took a moment to text her husband that she would be late getting home that evening. Then she huddled with the three detectives over sandwiches and coffee to come up with the broad analysis that the Chief had asked for. What had started as an ordinary unsolved mystery was turning into what might be the most intriguing case of all of their careers. She's taken a moment to text Damian on what was going on and checking his availability if questions came up during the meeting. She knew he had no desire to at all become any sort of public face for the case. He loved his privacy more than he loved fame. Fortunately, he was available to answer questions if she got stuck. The spreadsheet he's sent her contained the briefest summary of each case – death on a float, victim name, age, and police division, so they had enough information to work the case for the future.

With a few minutes to spare, they managed to put together some overhead slides that summarized the case. They were handwritten but legible and made a strong case. The four detectives left for the auditorium located on the first floor of police headquarters. There was a small group of outsiders that Natalie didn't recognize, and then a number of other police department personnel waiting for them. The Chief beckoned them to the front and then paused to make introductions before handing the presentation back to Sergeant Alvarez.

In a short time, she grabbed everyone's attention, given the size and the significance of the parade float death analysis. A few minutes later, questions were flying her way. She had Natalie take a turn at the podium to discuss how her single cold case had turned into a much larger problem. The police chief from Morgan Hill and his detective examined their city's case once they understood their parade death in the scheme of the bigger picture. They needed to go back and explore some of the findings from the death in their city four years ago.

The FBI Agent in Charge, Leticia Ortiz, had been madly

texting as soon as she understood the significance of the case. She stood up and walked to the front of the room to address the group.

"As you know, this case will be under the jurisdiction of the FBI. Crimes have occurred across multiple states as well as internationally. I'm not sure if I'll be leading the case, or if it will be someone else, but since the discovery started here, I'll do my best to keep the coordination of this case between the FBI and the San Jose Police Department. After all, this started because you wanted your cold case solved, and it will get solved. Detective Severino, you have an amazing civilian resource assisting you with your cold cases. Your chief was telling us a little about the cases you've solved with the help of the civilian. We'd like to interview him and potentially hire him to assist with this case."

"With all due respect Special Agent Ortiz, he'll be willing to talk with you, but not be hired by you. He has his hands in many pies, and my cold cases are just a minor use of his brain and computer power. Most of all, he does not want his name associated with this case. I'll give you his contact information, but don't be surprised by his lack of enthusiasm to join the team here."

"I'm sure I can convince him otherwise," the Special Agent said confidentially. "Meanwhile, I have resources coming in overnight from Quantico that will land at Moffett Field. I'd like us all to meet tomorrow morning at eight in our Palo Alto office. Does that work? Chief, I'm going to include our Public Relations person, and we need to discuss what we release to the press. I don't have high hopes of this case, staying quiet for long. From the data it appears we have had a killer at work for awhile, and the last thing we want to do is alert him or her to our awareness of these cases. I'd like to get a nod from everyone in this room, that the information we discussed today is confidential."

She then went around the room and waited for each person in attendance to give that nod. Natalie had to agree that catching the perpetrator would become much harder if word got out worldwide about his activity. It would also cause some parades to be canceled out of fear for the killer.

The meeting broke up after that. Natalie discussed verifying other murders overnight with Detectives Keil, Alvarez, and Rivera, but they might tip off another police department about the case, and it could leak from there. It was better to wait until the morning meeting. She provided Special Agent Ortiz with Damian's contact information, having alerted him to the agent's likely call. So far, she had several cold cases that were as interesting as any case she researched while being an active duty detective. She was driving home when she got a text from Damian indicating that he would dial into her meeting on a video chat to discuss his computer's projection about the Copenhagen Carnival.

CHAPTER 9

Hermione and Jacob plotted their tours of retail sites. Haley and Chris reviewed their plan and made minor corrections. Now the two teenagers were on the loose doing research for their future application.

"This job is so dope. My mom is lucky to work for Damian. She makes more money and comes home with more energy than she did when she worked at a café," Jacob said.

"I have to agree with you," Hermione said, as they sat in the backseat of a ride-share car on the way to their first store. "A few of my classmates are working in fast food, and their acne is getting worse being around all that grease. We have a lot of freedom and benefits, and when we're done, we don't smell like food. Did you show Damian the app and talk to him about your friend?"

"Yeah, I worked up the nerve to do it yesterday. Damian was pretty cool, and he played with the app. He asked for my friend's contact information. So we'll see what happens. I hope Jordan gets to join us."

Hermione didn't know what to think about an unknown person joining their team. She'd looked at this Jordan's app, and while she was impressed that he was earning a dollar on every download, it was an app for something she had no need of.

The two kids traveled around various cities for over three days collecting data. What seemed like a fun adventure at the start was dreary work by the second day. By the third day, there was a sigh of relief when their work was finished.

On the fourth day, they were organizing their findings to present to Chris and Haley when Damian approached the lab station.

"How did your retail store research go?"

"We are putting it together in a report for Chris and Haley, but I'll say that what started as an exciting adventure turned dull and boring midway through the first day of data collection," Hermione said.

Jacob added, "But we could see why it was necessary, which was part of the point of making us do that, right?"

Damian smiled and said, "Right. How can you create an application to fix something if you don't know what that something is? Besides, I usually discover something amongst all that boring research. Hopefully, you will too, that will make the application better. Jacob, I assumed you talk to Hermione about your friend Jordan?"

The boy nodded as Damian continued, "I spoke with him and his parents. I'm very impressed by him, and he will start next week. However, rather than helping you two, I have a new project for him to work on. Still, you'll have a third friend to hang out with at lunch."

Then he moved on to talk with other employees in the area.

Jacob said in a low voice to Hermione, "Score! I'm so excited that he's giving Jordan a chance. I wonder what project he's going to have him work on?"

"I don't know, Damian hasn't said anything to me. I know he has a lot of projects going on right now, and I'm not sure if he needs help with something in this warehouse or something outside of it. Oh well, we'll find out about it when we have lunch with Jordan."

The next week, Hermione met Jordan. She had several classmates named Jordan, and so she had visualized a composite of those classmates as to how Jordan looked. Now she could see she should've focused on the individual Jordans at her school. This Jordan looked similar to one of her high school basketball team players, then again, he didn't. The Jordan in front of her radiated intelligence. He was quiet but intense, yet awkward. He must've had a recent growth spurt that he hadn't quite settled into. He seemed clumsy because his body was taller than he remembered it to be. So he knocked things over with his hands and tripped over thresholds because he didn't pick his feet up enough. Hermione hoped that would get better for him in time, or maybe he would keep growing. She smiled at the thought of the food bill that would come from Jordan's employment.

Whatever Jordan was working on, was top-secret. The two teenagers had tried multiple angles to find out what it was. However, before he started, Damian had a long conversation with him about the consequences of saying anything to anyone. Jordan understood why he needed to keep his work secret, and he vowed to keep Damian's trust in him. It helped that Damian had warned him that the first questions would come from Hermione and Jacob. The second group of questions would come from his parents, and so Damian had worked out a response for Jordan to use that would stop the inquiries, but not give away the work he was doing. Damian had put Jordan in an empty cubicle so the teens could see that whatever he was doing, it was one-hundred percent computer work.

When Damian had reviewed Jordan's app, he did it out of courtesy to Jacob. He wasn't sure about the maturity level of the teenagers working for him. There were plenty of smart teenagers that he would love to hire, but he was a private person, and he wanted his company's work to be confidential until he said it was ready for public review.

In doing work with Natalie on the cold cases, he realized that he could help law enforcement everywhere by doing computer analysis of their crimes that remained unsolved. However, he needed a way to automate communication and computer work with those police departments. While Jordan's app was unrelated to law enforcement, Damian saw some similarities in the algorithm that might be used to create a law enforcement app. This application would sit atop their current information systems and do data searches for detectives in a way that wasn't happening now. Damian loved anything that put the bad guys behind bars, and if Jordan could design the app for him, he could contribute to putting more bad guys in jail.

Hermione and Jacob, their research completed, started working on the functionality of the app. They began by drawing a design of how they expected the app to work. Once they came to an agreement, they shared their genius with Haley and Chris. The two of them thought of an improvement to the process. Haley wanted the app user to know who was spying on them. Chris wanted an on/off switch so the app users could turn off the app inside certain aisles in the stores. This would enable the phone app user to still get store coupons in trade for releasing their shopping behavior information.

"Our first setback," Hermione said. "Our product wasn't perfect."

"It was perfect. There wasn't anything wrong with the design. It just could be more perfect with the changes they suggested," Jacob said, showing maturity beyond his years.

"Good point. I just thought of something else we should add. Let's set up a reward system so that our app users get badges with the more beacons they block. Maybe a badge for the first time the app was used, when our app has blocked ten beacons in a single store and so on. What do you think?"

"Mostly, I think badges are stupid. I'm going to do what I'm going to do for other reasons, not to earn a worthless virtual award. Still, in my view, dudes love badges, so yeah, let's add that feature. We'll have to think of cool names for the badges, so maybe we put that off to the side and work on it randomly between coding when our brains need a break."

"Good idea. You want to see if Jordan wants to go to lunch?"

Soon the three teens were seated at a table at Pete's restaurant. It wasn't as busy at lunch as it was at dinner, so usually, they had no wait to get a table. Hermione and Jacob had been at work two weeks longer than Jordan, but still, they loved the feeling of going to lunch on their own, ordering off the menu with no parental frowns, and having it put on the company's tab. There were other restaurants in the area that the company also had an arrangement with, and they would go explore those in time.

"Did Damian explain the food arrangement?" Hermione asked.

Jordan smiled and said, "All he said was the two of you would ask me to lunch on the first day and would explain the process to me. He was quite confident about that."

"And here we are, fulfilling his projection," Hermione said, unsure whether to be amused or annoyed at how predictable they were. She sighed and decided to spend lunch getting to know Jacob's friend.

CHAPTER 10

It had been a busy three weeks for Ariana. While Stefan had scrambled to find a new location for the fledgling company, she'd looked for additional funding and interim security to protect the company. Hermione had spent most evenings on the island with Damian, coming home on the weekend to stay with Ariana. It was an odd time, as she was used to having more time at home and the teenager in her life to share meals with. Still, she felt no guilt at putting long hours in to save Viramic.

Today, she would be at the company's location to help them pack and move to the new building. They had professional movers, but the scientists had rented a van with a generator to keep their research specimens in a steady state during the move. They didn't trust anyone to get it right but themselves. It was going to be a non-productive day for all of them, but once the move was over, their work would be secured. Stefan had found a location inside of another biotechnology company. The company had several buildings on its secured campus, one of which was unoccupied and perfectly suited to Viramic. After the move was accomplished today, the company would be physically secure, and it was just the scientists that would be at risk until they received their patent and began production of their virus protection vaccine.

Once production started, the financing would be better, and the scientists' safety would be secure as the research component would be done. The company's success would no longer be dependent on specific scientists.

As she was driving over the Golden Gate Bridge in the early dawn, her cell phone alarmed. She briefly glanced at it, thinking about where she could pull over on the road ahead. Just beyond the tollbooth, there was an area she could pull off.

She had just come to a stop when there was an incoming call from Damian.

"I know, I know my company alarm is going off. I just crossed the bridge and needed to come to a stop so I could handle the problem. What do you know?"

"Bad news I'm afraid. The fire department is on the way there as someone threw explosives at the building. It broke the glass but bounced back once it hit the plywood behind the glass. I have the camera feed, so I can see some of the action, but some of the cameras were knocked out. There are cars nearby that were damaged."

"Crap. Do you see anyone injured nearby? Is the building still standing?"

Ariana knew that she could pull up the video feed on her own phone, but she presumed that Damian was calling from home, and had a bigger screen to view the explosion with. He could get her answers faster than she could.

"I don't see anyone injured, and the building looks damaged, but not structurally. Is anyone at work there at this hour? Isn't this the day you are planning on moving?"

"Yes, and this is going to delay us and keep us in this vulnerable location longer."

Ariana had shared the moving plan with Damian during one of their dinners.

"If I were you, I would get the actual research into your rented van today and move that. The furniture and lab equipment can wait until tomorrow. You're going to be tied up with the police and fire departments as your building is a crime scene now, but perhaps with a lot of explanations and a police escort, you could move your research to the new location. I'll get off the phone now so you can talk to the company, but at least you know what's going on."

She thanked him and ended the call, dialing Stefan Weiss.

"You heard the alarm?" he asked when their call connected.

"Yes. I know the company was bombed, and police and fire are on their way. I'm just over the Golden Gate Bridge, so I'll be there in an hour or less depending on traffic. Damian said the building would become a crime scene, but to see if we could move the research portion in our van with the police escort today, and leave the other stuff to move when we're cleared by the police. Are you at the building?"

"I can't get to it as the streets are blocked. I'm going to park my car, and then Julia and I will walk the rest of the way."

"Is your security escort with you?" Ariana asked, with concern in her voice.

"Yes."

"Talk to them as to whether you're safe leaving your car unattended. They also need to protect you on the walk, and out in the open while you speak to the emergency responders. So stay safe, and I'll see you soon," Ariana suggested, trying not to be too paranoid.

She heard nothing more about the event as she finished her drive south. She tuned into several radio stations, but either they weren't talking about it yet, or she was missing the broadcast by skipping around the channels. Much like Stefan mentioned, she found the streets around the building blocked, and so she sought parking, planning to hoof it the final half a mile. Police blocked her at the barricade until Stefan was reached, her identity verified, and she was allowed to pass under the police tape. As she walked toward the building, she saw Stefan and Julia ahead. Again she worried about their safety in the open like this, but the police barricades kept people pretty far from them.

"Hey guys, what's happened since we talked?" Ariana asked once she was within speaking distance.

"I spoke with the arson expert from the fire department, and he confirmed what we saw on the video. It was an arson. The police are involved and want to interview you and Damian. There isn't much damage to the building or the company. Thankfully, we put that thick plywood behind the windows last week, or we would have suffered a lot more damage. The fire person says the bombs exploded on contact with the plywood, but they offered enough of a barrier that they bounced backward, and outside rather than inside. However, someone knew our floor plan, as the targeted rooms are closest to the research specimens. Whoever threw the bombs at the building picked certain windows as they had the possibility to do more damage," Stefan said.

"Where would they have gotten that information?" asked Ariana.

"The fire inspector said they could have walked into our building, or from a cleaning service, from county records, or from one of our employees."

"I think we have to rule out the first two as we have long had security preventing anyone from entering the interior of the company, and we don't have a cleaning service," Julia said. "I hate to think that one of our own employees snitched on us, so that leaves public records."

"Except that we just had walls installed. We use bio-safety cabinets with HEPA filters without ducts to the outside, so anyone looking at our plans would be unable to determine which rooms contained valuable experiments. Sadly, that means they have an internal source."

Ariana paused to think about Stefan's words and examine the

scene in front of her. Then she asked, "Will the police escort you while you move the research specimens?"

"Yes, they will. I had a long conversation with a Captain who has responsibility for bombs and hazardous materials. We'll get a full-on police escort to our new location in South San Francisco for the van. I think they're happy to be rid of us. I'm just waiting for the fire department and crime scene units to give us the all-clear to go inside and start moving stuff."

"Where are your employees?" Ariana asked, looking around.

"Since we're only moving the research specimens, Julia and I will handle it, so I gave them all a paid day off. If one of them is a spy, I don't want to give them other opportunities to sabotage the company's specimens today," Stefan said.

"Do you have any idea of how to figure out who is the problem employee?" Julia asked.

"I know that Damian researched all of the employees as part of his security check-up for the company. Let me see if he has any guesses, and they will be guesses, as none of them was particularly suspicious when he did his analysis a few weeks ago. Meanwhile, do you have any idea of when you can start moving? I'm here to help," Ariana asked.

Stefan suddenly seemed to notice that she wasn't in her usual business attire of a nice pantsuit or casual dress. Instead, she was in sneakers, jeans, and a t-shirt suitable for someone helping to move.

"They said they had another hour of collecting evidence, then we can move stuff from our specimen lab to the van. One of our security detail stayed with the van to make sure nothing happened to it, and the police will allow it inside the perimeter once a few fire trucks clear away."

Ariana looked around, counting in her head, and then pulled out her phone. "I'll order donuts and coffee for about thirty people. It will be our thanks for the police escort and their work today. We just need to borrow a table from inside the building, so we have space to set it on."

"I know of a folding table in one of our rooms, I'll go fetch it now," Stefan said, walking over to the officer closest to the entrance for a short conversation. He returned with a table, and Stefan, Julia, and Ariana, once the refreshments arrived, made friends with all of the first responders who had come to their rescue.

The Captain returned to their little group to give them a status. "You'll be able to begin loading your specimens shortly if you want to bring your vehicle here. I'd also recommend getting a handy person to put some plywood over your openings to secure your building."

"I've already contacted the person who put it up in the first place, and he will come once they're cleared to do so. I sent him pictures of the damage so he would know what to buy. Will he be allowed inside now?"

"Yes, if he explains to my men what he is here to do and has plywood in his possession, then he'll be allowed through. We're going to collapse our barrier around your building to just this street in a little bit, and it will remain in place till sometime tomorrow. Now, another question, we have the news media here asking questions. Given what you've told us may be in play here, we don't want to say that to the media. This is what I'm prepared to say. 'We have evidence that explosives were thrown at this building. The only occupant is a biotech firm that is ending its lease of the building this week. While we have video of the suspects that threw the explosives, we as yet do not have any identified suspects, and the public is not at risk.' Do you have a desire to comment?"

"No. I have nothing to add other than I'm grateful that none of my employees were injured."

"Okay, I'll add that to the statement," the Captain said, making notes as he walked away.

"I hadn't thought of the media," Ariana said. "We definitely don't want to share our suspicions with them. Still, I bet you get calls."

"My response to that is the explosion destroyed our phone lines," Stefan said with a small smile. "You got to use it as an excuse where you can."

Soon, a man got out of a pick-up truck that pulled as close as he could without getting in the way of the firetrucks. He walked up to Stefan and said, "We're ready to install the plywood when you're ready."

Stefan looked at the woman he knew was in charge of the crime scene, and she held up five fingers in response to his question about how much longer.

Stefan's handyman and his associate began unloading wood and stacking it close to the building where it was close to the openings, but not in the way of the first responders.

Julia went with the protection detail to move the van in close for loading, once the firetruck in front of the building left. She soon returned, and they checked the generator that was supposed to keep the temperature inside in perfect conditions for their specimens during the move. By early afternoon, the building was sealed, and their little convoy was on the move to their new location.

Ariana had never visited the biotech district in South San Francisco. There was no security gate to reach the multitude of pharmaceutical companies, but the buildings were so big, that simply throwing explosives at one of them wouldn't necessarily hit the target. Ariana helped them move into the portion of the building they were leasing. Then they went to talk to the security for the building.

CHAPTER 11

Natalie arrived at the FBI building for their scheduled meeting full of excitement at the thought of catching someone who was an evil person. She knew that the FBI and the command structure at the SJPD would remove it from her hands; she was a retired detective, after all, dabbling in cold cases. Still thanks to Damian, she was establishing a heck of a closure rate. She was also excited when Damian told her confidentially that he was creating a computer app so that more departments could be helped by using his immense computing power. She was anxious to see what would come from this meeting. She entered the meeting room and was warmly greeted by everyone she knew. The Chief had worked out a meeting agenda with his counterpart from the FBI, and Natalie was first up describing how her early work on the case had got her to today's meeting.

The Chief opened the meeting with introductions then gave the floor to Natalie. She silently passed loads of respect his way. He could have easily excluded her from the meeting and had her Lieutenant give this presentation, but using the closest source to a situation was essential to him.

"I'm retired Detective Severino, and I've been working on cold cases for my old department. We had an unsolved parade float murder case dating back fifteen years ago. As any detective would do, I updated all of the players in the case. I have a friend who provides data analyses on some of these cold cases."

The Chief interrupted her with, "She has a higher solve rate in her retirement than she did on the force and her data friend helped us reunite a child with her parents, found some bank robbers that got away with $60M, and shut down some very bad gang members in San Quentin."

Natalie appreciated the Chief's support and privately reminded herself to thank the Lieutenant later.

"Yes, when I contacted him, I thought we would be able to reconstruct who the murderer was by having his computer sort through thousands of pictures taken at the parade. That proved to be a bad idea as the time sort of the photos depended on where the photographer stood in a three-mile parade route. Still, my data friend did a search of other deaths by poison dart for the five years around my cold case and found almost none. Then he thought to do a search of deaths on parade floats, and he hit the jackpot. We then expanded his search to the last twenty years and hit the mother lode. Someone is dying on a float about every three weeks around the world."

Natalie paused to see if anyone had questions while she looked at the audience's faces. No one put their hand up.

"Obviously, some of these deaths really are accidents. People can be run over or fall off a float leading to a fatal injury. Yesterday we did a sample of fifteen cases around the United States and determined that at least twelve were suspicious. That was when the Chief put the call into the FBI. We also had one other unsolved float death case in a nearby city–Morgan Hill."

Now someone did interrupt her by asking, "You're saying you have a list of nearly two-hundred-fifty float deaths over the past twenty years?"

"Yes. Furthermore, I asked my data guy if his computer could project where the next murder would be–in what upcoming parade will our murderer find his next victim?"

Natalie heard conversation break out over her last sentence, and so she continued.

"The next projected murder is at the Copenhagen Carnival, which occurs at the end of this week in Denmark. However, my data guy feels that his computer is only forty-percent accurate in the projection. He considers that to be a low accuracy rate. If we could eliminate the cases off this list that were truly accidents, we would have a higher accuracy rate."

"If the projection is correct, though, we don't have enough time to correct the list, especially as we're dealing with language barriers and international locations," said Special Agent in Charge Leticia Ortiz. "We can't just call a police force in Tanzania, and expect to determine if a case is a murder or an accident in an hour or so. Some of these locations may not have enough tools to determine the difference."

"Certainly even if I devoted all of my detective division to this case, it would take us weeks to have a better list," the Chief said.

"I think I need to make some calls to my colleagues in Copenhagen and with Interpol in New York City. Did your data guy give you any additional projections for the next murder? I assume Copenhagen was tops but were there other cities with parades with an even lower probability?"

Natalie took a brief look at her notes to examine her notes on Copenhagen.

"He did not, but I'm sure he could run that or any additional data."

"Do you or he have any other comments about the raw data?" Ortiz asked.

"He commented that there appeared to be deaths on boat parades in addition to street parades."

"Interesting and how unfortunate that there are so many

parades throughout the world," Ortiz said. "Our most recent float death was a few weeks ago in Mexico during a Cinco de Mayo parade, correct?"

"Yes."

"My team would like to discuss the next steps, you're all welcome to listen in and contribute. The Behavioral Analysis Unit will put together a profile on our suspect. Detective Severino, I assume you feel the next step to solving your cold case lies in Copenhagen."

"I do. I think with additional resources, we could develop more details about the float deaths that might give us a clue as to which float the killer might pick. There are two-thousand parade participants, some on floats, some dancing in the streets. If we're going to focus on that parade, then we still need to limit our focus."

"That's an excellent suggestion Detective. We'll add that to the to-do list."

Natalie listened in on the conversation and liked Agent Ortiz's process to devise a plan to tackle this case. She was impressed up to the moment the Agent planned on using the FBI's data analysis unit rather than Damian, and she couldn't stay silent.

"Look, this is a huge case with a potential ticking time bomb in the Copenhagen Carnival. I think you would be foolish to use anyone other than my data guy to get you what you need over the next forty-eight hours. After all, his supercomputers out-performed the FBI's in discovering this trend of homicides," Natalie said, and then wondered if she was going to be dressed down for disrespect. Oh well, she definitely felt like she had more freedom to speak as a retired officer.

There was silence in the room, and Natalie snuck a glance at her department, to find that they were all hiding small smiles. Okay, she wasn't going to be fired today.

"Detective, I've never worked with your data guy, so I don't have the faith that you do. Furthermore, he declined to appear at this meeting, whereas I have a department IT representative here."

"True, but he does run his own company, and his presence wasn't critical to this meeting," Natalie said, knowing for sure her pink slip was coming.

"Can you arrange a meeting with him in an hour?" the Agent asked.

"Possibly, though, it might take more than an hour to reach his location, depending on where he is. Overall, he's very interested in supporting the arrest of criminals as his family was murdered by a mistakenly released inmate from Soledad prison. So he'll try to meet your needs as long as we don't waste his time. I'll go call him," she said, stepping out of the meeting room.

Yep, this was the last cold case that the SJPD would allow her to work on. They probably thought she didn't respect authority. However, in her world, Damian Green was more important to her than the FBI. She dialed his number, thankful that he picked up the call.

"Hi, Damian. Where are you physically at the moment? The head of the local office of the FBI wants to meet with you as soon as possible."

"I'm in my warehouse in Richmond. It will take you at least an hour to drive here."

"Maybe I can get the SJPD to fly us to you. Is there a helicopter pad somewhere close by if they take that option?"

Damian thought about the neighborhood and replied, "If folks don't mind a two-block walk, there's an empty field they can put down in close by," and he gave the address.

Natalie ended the call and returned inside. Her suggestion of the police helicopter was met with frowns. Still, twenty minutes later, she found herself climbing into the helicopter with her Lieutenant's Captain, Agent Ortiz, and two of her people. She asked the pilot what the ETA was and texted Damian, who planned to meet them at the field.

After a beautiful flight across the bay, they landed in the field that Damian mentioned. The pilot would stay with the helicopter as he could be called away by an emergency. Natalie led the way toward Damian, and introductions were performed.

"If you'll follow me, we'll be at my office soon."

"What kind of work do you do?" Ortiz asked.

"This and that. I'm an inventor, so I pursue whatever interests me. I'm also a software designer, so I do a lot of geeky projects," Damian said, deciding that he would share with everyone the project that he had Jordan working on. He knew the kid was tired of evading everyone's questions.

The group followed him upstairs to where his staff was working on various projects. He headed toward Jordan as his little group looked around at the gadgets that people were playing with.

He called over his team and ignoring his guests, he said to them, "You've all been curious about what Jordan has been working on, and so I decided to share it with you and the FBI at the same time. Jordan here is working on a smartphone app to provide a portal to law enforcement to do some of the searches I now do for Natalie. I could help you guys solve more crimes if I had more time, so I'm removing me, the middleman, so you can do your searches in a friendlier way than currently exists for law enforcement."

He heard Hermione and Jacob say 'cool' and 'that's dope' in reaction to Jordan's job.

"Will there be a charge for the app?" asked Natalie's Captain.

"Yes. I want Jordan to make some money on his invention, and there are a limited number of cop shops to sell the app to. So I'm thinking about the price of two-ninety-nine."

Jordan looked up and smiled as one of Natalie's party asked, "Two hundred ninety-nine? Our budget can probably support that."

"No, two-dollars and ninety-nine cents. There are over seventeen thousand police agencies in the United States, which will contribute a little over fifty-thousand to Jordan's college fund."

"Wow," breathed Hermione and Jacob, thinking about having that kind of cash for college.

"Wow," said each of Natalie's party, amazed at the affordability of such an app.

Natalie's Captain said to Jordan, "If this app is as good as Mr. Green describes, forget police departments, you'll have half of the uniformed police, about four-hundred thousand buying your app. Now, that's my kind of a college fund. You'll enter college as a millionaire."

"I don't want to wreck Jordan's life, so we'll figure out some other pricing strategy that doesn't make him a millionaire," Damian replied. "So what brings you folks here today?"

"Natalie was quite convinced that you would be the faster source for information on our current case," Ortiz said. Then realizing there were three teenagers present, she asked, "Do you think we might find a private table in the restaurant on the first floor of this building?"

Damian looked at his watch and replied, "Sure, we have about forty-two minutes before the lunch rush arrives. Follow me."

Soon they were settled with lunch ordered, "Okay, there are no kids around, and we ordered our food; what do you need from me?"

"I was going to ask our IT department in West Virginia to do some more modeling with your data, but Natalie says it would be faster if we used you. Even though you only gave us a forty percent probability with Copenhagen, we're going to focus on that parade. There are two-thousand entrants, so we need to narrow our focus to just a few floats. Can you help us with that?"

"Sure," Damian said, taking out his mobile phone. He tapped a few things, and then his computer was going to work on the Agent's question. Once he saw the program engage, he said, "We should have the result in twenty-three minutes."

"This, I've got to see," was all Agent Ortiz could say, with apparent disbelief written across her face.

Damian smiled faintly at her reaction, while Natalie was full of affront at what she saw as disrespect by the agent.

The captain ignored the swirling emotions at the table and returned to the topic of Jordan's app with questions about how it would work. Nearly all of the law enforcement systems required logins to access data. How could an app help with searches given the password necessary to access them? Damian explained the process over lunch. They were just finishing their meal when his phone vibrated.

Damian viewed his phone and said, "The report is ready. Let's return upstairs so I can print it out for you."

In silence, they returned to Damian's office, each looking at a copy his computer had produced. It didn't tell them which float, but significantly limited which float it would be. The person to die would be covered head to toe in a costume. As the Copenhagen Carnival was a celebration of samba and other Latin American dances, the vast majority of floats had dancers, not costumed characters. Based on the previous year's parade, this finding would limit the parade floats to three floats.

The FBI's computer person said, "Special Agent Ortiz, I could not have done as well as Mr. Green did in giving you answers. I would suggest you use him as a resource whenever he allows it. I'm not sure how you gained access to the world's law enforcement systems, but clearly, as you're using it to do good, I'm not going to worry about it. Perhaps after this case is over, he might indulge me in some training?"

"Call me, and we'll arrange that," Damian replied.

CHAPTER 12

As was their habit, the three teenagers would go to lunch by themselves. Eating with the adults was fine, but it was like eating with your parents. They had tried everything on Pete's menu, and now they were going to try a restaurant two blocks away for the first time. They were busy discussing their results from a video game, and how if they were the software designer, they would add certain features. That conversation carried them all the way to the restaurant, and the three of them felt like they entered adulthood for paying for their lunch with their paycheck earnings.

After years of being watchful and secretive, first living with her parents, and then in the initial stages with Damian and Ariana, Hermione was more observant than your average teenager. She noticed that a man and woman were seated next to them in the restaurant. However, there were many other open tables, and she thought she had seen them signal to the hostess to sit at that table. Then she listened for a conversation coming from the other table and didn't hear anything. Jacob and Jordan continued their discussion, and Hermione found she could stay out of it and concentrate on the other table. At one point, she glanced over her shoulder, thinking maybe the two were using their cell phones instead of talking with one another. Still, when she glanced around as if assessing the restaurant, she noted that there were no cell phones on their table. How strange? Why would they dine together and then not talk to each other?

Hermione decided to hold her phone up like she was using the selfie function to put lip gloss on and snap a photo of the people behind her. Jacob and Jordan looked at her in horror as if wondering when she had morphed into a girl? She took a look at the photo she snapped and was satisfied that she captured the two people. Shortly afterwards, they left the restaurant to return to work. About a block away from the restaurant, Hermione stopped the guys so she could see what the couple did.

"Why are you acting so strange?" Jacob finally asked.

"Call me paranoid, but the couple at the table next to us were listening in on our conversation. So, while you guys were frowning at my usage of lip gloss, I was actually taking a picture of the couple. I want to see where they go."

"Paranoid," Jacob said.

"What?" asked Hermione, watching the restaurant's exit.

"You said to call you paranoid, so I did because you are."

"Oh. See, they're leaving now in deep conversation and heading our way. Hurry, let's get back to the office. They didn't talk at all during lunch, and then they have a robust conversation once we leave. I don't think so."

Jacob and Jordan just continued to give her rolled eyes mixed with disbelief, and they returned to the office without incident.

Hermione waited until she was riding home with Damian that night to tell him about the odd couple at lunch.

"We went to the restaurant in the strip mall for lunch today. I noticed that this couple sat next to us in a mostly empty restaurant and that they didn't talk at all. It felt like they were listening in to our conversation because as soon as we left and got about a block away, they soon exited the restaurant. At one point, I checked, and it wasn't because they were involved with their phones."

"That does sound strange. What else did the couple do that you noticed?"

"So you think I'm paranoid too. That's what Jacob and Jordan said."

"No, I don't think that as your watchfulness and street smarts have kept you alive, and out of someone's custody. I'm just not sure what I can do about a random couple. I think we closed the book on all of your parents' enemies."

"I pretended to put lip gloss on, and took a selfie that was mostly them, so I was hoping you could identify them."

"Kiddo, sometimes you are way too mature for your tender years. Yes, I'll see if I can identify the couple," Damian said, smiling at the teenager as he pulled into his parking space at the marina. "This could take awhile. Do you want to stay here overnight, or would you rather head to Ariana's place now, and I'll call you when I have something?"

"I'll let Ariana know I'm staying here tonight. I want to watch what you do to run down these people. Maybe if they're nobodies, I can relax. Or maybe my parents failed to mention another enemy of theirs."

The two of them stepped into his speedy boat for the less than five-minute ride to Red Rock Island. Once there, Damian pulled the boat inside his boat garage along with the dock. As they walked into the lower level of the house, Damian said, "Send me the photo in question."

Like any teenager, she walked around with the phone in her hands, so it was a matter of seconds before the phone made the sound of an outgoing text. Damian stopped at his lab computer and opened Hermione's photo, and then entered it into his facial identity system. It wasn't the best photo like a mug shot, or driver's license might be, but it was all they had.

Hermione leaned on the raised table supporting Damian's computer and watched it think.

"Will this take long?" she asked.

"It shouldn't. Do you remember anything else about the couple like were they American?"

Just then, the computer changed to a different picture of the couple. Hermione read, "Shelly Monson and Michael Swatten. No criminal convictions, and it says they work for Consolidated Security Systems. What kind of company is that? Does it have anything to do with my parents?"

"I don't know. Let's get some more information," Damian said, clicking away on his keyboard to do just that.

"So this company provides a wide range of security services. I wonder if they're private investigators. Let me see if I can find a P.I. license for them in the state database."

"So it's probably related to my parents," Hermione said, sighing.

"Let's not make that conclusion yet," Damian said while searching the PI license database. "Ah, here they are. I don't remember any of your parents' enemies hiring American investigators to track you. Let me see if I can find out who some of the clients are for Consolidated Security Systems. Do you want to head upstairs and start preparing dinner?"

"No. I want to watch what you're doing, so the next time I feel suspicious about people, I can do my own search."

"You can do that, but I would rather you tell Ariana or me if someone is making you uncomfortable."

"This may be some childhood neurosis stemming from living with my parents, and then with you and Ariana, that I'm never going to outgrow."

"Whoa, that's a whole lot of psychological analysis. I don't think you're neurotic about strangers as you don't feel that way about every stranger you meet. I would look at it as 'you're very sensitive to people around you', and that's not such a bad thing if your gut is more often right than wrong."

"That's another way to look at it. Let's see if my gut is right about these two people. How are you going to figure out who their clients are? Do they list that on a website?"

"Some companies do, but I would guess, in this case, that discretion would stop them from posting. I'm going to search for some of their documents like annual reports, tax filings, and other statements. Basically, I'm asking the computer to round up any information in cyberspace about this company and collect it for me. After dinner, I'll look at what it has found."

"What if it doesn't find anything?" Hermione asked, worried about not being able to solve the mystery of these two people and her gut reaction to them.

"If all else fails, I'll attempt to hack into their databases and see what I can find."

Hermione grinned at his response and said, "Let's go fix dinner. Do we need to fish for Bailey and Bella?"

"We do. Why don't you do that while I get supper going? I have some chicken breasts that I'll do on the barbecue, couscous, and corn. If you need dessert, there are cookies or ice cream."

"Sounds like a plan," Hermione said, heading into her bedroom to drop off her backpack and change from sandals to shoes as she didn't want to slip on the cliff edge of the island while she fished.

Forty minutes later, Damian was in his kitchen, putting the final touches on their dinner. Hermione had quickly caught fresh fish for the cats that would last them the next three days. Damian sliced up the fish as Hermione didn't have the heart to kill the fish even though she had caught them for the express purpose of feeding them to the cats.

A while later, with dinner completed and cleaned up, they each grabbed a cookie and returned downstairs to Damian's lab to see what his computer had collected.

Damian scanned the readout and then passed it to Hermione.

"See if you find a problem here."

Hermione looked at the five pages that consisted of names of people and companies and then shook her head.

"I don't see anything here."

Damian smiled and said, "I'm going to train you to be a little bit of a detective. What project are you working on for me?"

Hermione was puzzled with the question and said, "You know what I do; you assigned it to me."

"Yes, I did. There's a name on these pages that relates to that assignment. Here, study the list again."

Hermione thought about Damian's clue and then grabbed a marker to cross out the names of individuals. She and Jacob had collected no individual names related to their app. Was it a store they had visited? She looked for those names and didn't see them on the page. She went through the pages three more times and then arrived on a name, 'BlueSilver Company'.

"It's the BlueSilver Company, isn't it?"

"Yes. You and Jacob must have been observed collecting data about the store beacons, and now people are watching you. I'm going to call Lily so we can all discuss this situation, okay?"

"Yeah, we should do that," Hermione sighed, and then added, "I must be genetically predisposed to trouble."

Damian hugged her and said, "You are all the wiser for all this trouble. Neither Jacob nor Jordan saw the trouble sitting at the next table. That will serve you well in life."

Hermione sighed again as Damian called Lily.

"Hi, Lily. Do you have a minute for a conversation?"

Lily was puzzled by the call as she couldn't think of when Damian had called her before at home in the evening.

"Is something wrong?"

"Maybe, is Jacob available to join Hermione and I on the call?"

"What did that boy do?"

"Lily, you know Jacob is a good kid. We've got a complication with the app they're developing, and I think he and Hermione and you need to be a part of the discussion."

"Oh, okay, just a moment."

They heard her yell Jacob's name, asking him to join her on a phone call with Damian and Hermione. That was an excellent way to get the teenager's attention.

"Okay, we're both here. What's going on?"

"Jacob, Jordan, and Hermione went out to lunch today to that Thai restaurant two blocks away. Hermione noticed that a couple came in and sat at the table next to them, but never talked themselves, nor were they staring at their phones. That unnerved her, and so she took a selfie of herself, that was really of the couple."

"Yeah, she told Jordan and me about them, but we just called her paranoid," Jacob said. In the background, they heard Lily admonished him, 'Jacob!'.

"Turns out she wasn't paranoid. The couple is a pair of private detectives that I think have been hired by the BlueSilver Company, one of the makers of store beacons."

"What the heck!" asked Lily. "How dare they target children!"

Damian could feel the eyes rolling of both teenagers even though he couldn't see Jacob.

"Now that you got your indignation out, let's talk about what we are going to do," Damian said with a smile in his voice.

"Do you think the kids are at risk?" Lily asked, going straight to the heart of the matter.

"I don't know. I don't know if these people are collecting information about their habits and whereabouts, or if they're listening in to see what Hermione and Jacob are saying about the app design. I think we have to prepare for the worst and hope for the best.

"What's best?" Lily asked.

"It was just a chance meeting between the couple and the kids."

"But you don't believe that," Lily said.

"I'm trusting Hermione's gut instinct on this one. The kids, at the very least, are being tracked, so let us talk about protecting them."

"How about if they quit their jobs?" Lily asked.

There were shouts on both ends of the phone by Hermione and Jacob, a thunderous and extended 'no'.

"I guess that means you guys like your jobs?" Damian said with a smile in his voice.

There was a chorus of 'yes' 'the job is dope' in reply.

"Lily, I also think my company is at risk as they don't know who all is working on the app and how far they have gotten. I think we should discuss this at work tomorrow first thing, but let's talk about your safety tonight and tomorrow. Why don't Hermione and I pick you up and take you to work? Do you have an alarm on your house?"

"Are you kidding? Did you forget I did time for a bank robbery? I bet I have a better house alarm than you do, Damian, and yes to the ride."

"Do you have water cannons and bulletproof windows?" asked Hermione.

"What?" Jacob asked, immense disbelief in his voice.

"Forgive me, Damian, I forgot who I was talking to. You're right, you have a better security system. Jacob and I will talk over solutions, and we'll see you at eight?" Lily said, guessing on a pick-up time.

"See you at eight. Stay safe," Hermione said as the call ended.

CHAPTER 13

General Yong-ho was very displeased to learn of the failure of bombing Viramic's laboratories in the United States. The Marshal would soon replace him if he didn't have results. That was the way things went; you either did your job well or you were replaced. However, he planned this operation as a gift to the Marshal and as an example of the General's leadership. It was time to visit Lee Nak-yon to see what his hacker had learned. Surely, he'd learned something new by now. Subtle solutions weren't working, it might be time to eliminate key members of the company. It wasn't big, and not everyone needed to be dead.

The General's car arrived at the factory where Lee had his office. The CEO knew he was coming, and so the General hoped that by setting an arrival time, he would put pressure on Lee to come up with something by the appointed time.

Lee Nak-yon hated these visits by the General, but the man was powerful, and Lee couldn't afford to anger him. He had new information that he purposely was slow in passing on. Lee was always an honest businessman, and he hated the political games played by his government. It was a waste of time and money.

He stood and bowed and waited for the man to take a seat.

"What do you have for me?"

"My best hacker gave me new information just an hour ago. The American company knows that someone from North Korea is trying to enter their computer systems. He also said the systems were down because the building the company was located in caught fire today. Some of the employees went home, and a smaller group moved critical experiments to a new location. I have the location address for you," Lee said, passing a piece of paper to the General.

"Is that all you have? My other sources already gave me that information."

"General Yong-ho, I also learned that one of the company's employees has family in Dandong, China, close to our border. She sends them money, so I bet you could threaten the family and gain leverage with the employee. She's not a scientist, but she would be able to tell us how close the company is to publishing scientific results. Would that be helpful?"

The General looked interested when he heard that bit of news. Finally, some leverage against the company. He needed to know how he could stop this company. A small part of him worried that it was already too late. He would launch his infectious Agent, and a month later, the West would have an antidote for the infection, and relatively few people would die. His weapon of mass destruction would be laughed at by the other generals, and he would spend the rest of his days up north in a work camp.

"Now, you're talking. We will find a way to reach this woman after we move her family from China to here. We can pull the family across the border. Nothing like being moved to North Korea to frighten people."

"Very good, Sir. Here's the woman's name and the name of the family and address in Dandong," Lee said, hoping the General would depart and leave him alone.

"I want to continue to keep track of our man in the company. Can you send me daily updates?"

"Yes, sir."

The General left his office, and Lee sighed as he always did when the menacing presence left his office. He always looked out his window and toward the south, where the border was between North and South Korea. It was so close, yet so far away.

CHAPTER 14

Leticia Ortiz invited Natalie Severino to join her in a meeting in Washington DC. They were in their descent into Reagan National Airport. First, she had to get her agency on board, as the case had started in her region but had national and international implications. She admitted that it would be quite the gold star on top of an already stellar career. She knew that if she wanted to move higher in the FBI, she would have to relocate to Virginia or Washington DC. She liked where she lived now, and the West Coast had strange enough cases to keep her interest in the job alive. She was gathering civilian contacts that landed her unique cases and took some terrible people off the streets. She'd assisted a private forensic pathologist in her area by the name of Dr. Jill Quint with some cases. She suspected that after the computer talent she had seen from Damian Green, the abilities of the three of them combined would be an unstoppable crime-solving team.

"We'll head to the Hoover building for a meeting, and then we'll likely wait around while we try to meet with the Royal Danish Embassy Representatives. Also, we have an FBI agent tied to the American Embassy in Copenhagen, and so we'll connect with them as well. You'll be repeating yourself as you'll be describing this case several times over the upcoming hours."

"I appreciate my department sending me as a representative to these meetings. It's exciting to connect with all of these law enforcement agencies worldwide. Of course, each new person might decide that this case is just too far-fetched," Natalie replied.

"I've worked on some other foreign cases, and our agency has a pretty good reputation, so I don't think you'll meet much resistance. Besides, why wouldn't the Danes want to solve another float murder in their country?"

In their review of the list of float deaths, there had been an earlier one in Denmark. During the Christmas parade in Aarhus, someone dressed in a gnome costume was found dead by the end of the parade. The death was called an accident, but there were unanswered questions.

Natalie smiled and moved through the terminal with the agent. Soon they were in a taxi, their carry-on bags stowed in the trunk. The agent said they would be gone overnight, and possibly longer advising the Detective to pack a carry-on containing as many changes of clothing as she could fit, and to bring her passport. They left their weapons at home as the agent hinted that they might continue on to Denmark, and they wouldn't want to take the time to get permission to bring guns into the country.

Natalie had been to Washington DC before but hadn't stopped at the Hoover building. She heard there was an enjoyable tour, but as far as she was concerned, she was getting the visit of her life alongside Special Agent in Charge Ortiz. Natalie guessed she was fifteen years older than the agent and was happy to see more respect for female law enforcement officials, than at the start of her career.

There were two division heads from the FBI that would coordinate their response, the International Operations and the Critical Incident Response Group that consisted of behavioral analysts. Once Natalie discussed her cold case, and how it had expanded to what appeared to be a global serial killer, she was hit with many questions. Was her data valid, how could someone have the resources and time to travel the world killing people and other issues? Agent Ortiz ran interference for her, allowing her to get back to the most significant assumption of all – the next murder was likely to occur within the next three days during a carnival in Copenhagen.

Shortly, the Ambassador and her entourage arrived from the Royal Embassy of Denmark. Natalie's explanation started all over again, but the Ambassador was native to Aarhus and remembered the parade participant's death. She was quick to grasp the situation and come on board to facilitate a meeting between the FBI and the Copenhagen police. It was late in the evening in Denmark. She made arrangements for Leticia, Natalie, and herself to meet with the police the next morning. The FBI charted a jet to take them overnight to the Danish capital. Natalie thought briefly about the CIA being involved, but decided this was outside of their scope.

Natalie was texting Damian with each step that the story traveled up the law enforcement food chain. He cheered her on while she told him he was unknowingly making friends in high places. Damian was content to stay in the background, provide any data that Natalie needed, and make sure all the kudos landed on her back.

Their little group was hustled through Danish Immigration and Customs, thanks to the Ambassador and the Copenhagen Chief Constable's greasing of the wheels. Natalie felt like she was living the dream life of a law enforcement agent; she was on the trail of a serial killer. Then she mentally slapped her face and told herself to put her feet back on the ground. The brilliance was Damian's; he was the one that thought of the way to look at the data.

After introductions, which were all in English, they sat around a large conference table and waited for Natalie to begin her explanation.

"I'm a retired detective from the San Jose, California police department. My city has about 1,100 officers, but in my retirement, I work to clear cold cases for the department. As you know, new DNA enters our systems every day. I am fortunate to have assistance from a civilian with impressive access to and analysis of data. My cold case is a woman who was in full costume and was shot with a poisonous dart while on a parade float. That case occurred more than a decade ago and has never been solved. I asked my data guy to search for poison dart murders, and we didn't get anything relevant. He then took a look at deaths on parade floats, and there's quite a pattern there. Here's a map of where float deaths have occurred over the past twenty years or so," Natalie posted a map of the murder locations on a computer projector. "You will see that you've had one here in the city of Aarhus. Some of these deaths indeed are accidents or heart attacks. My colleagues and I studied fifteen cases in the U.S., and based on that sampling, roughly eighty-percent of the cases may be the work of this killer."

"So this is about a case in Aarhus?" interrupted Police Constable Oliver Nielsen.

"No. We asked one more question of our data person. We asked for a projection of where he or she would strike next. The answer is on one of about three floats at the Copenhagen Carnival this weekend."

This pronouncement was greeted by dead silence in the room. Natalie felt as if she could hear the Danish voices screaming out loud 'What!'. Then she smiled slightly at the fanciful voice in her head. 'What' was an English word. They would be screaming the Danish equivalent.

"You better give us more explanation," the Constable said, after the long, silent pause in the room.

Natalie took more time and explained the timing of a variety of deaths that had occurred over the past twenty years, the low probability provided by the computer given that some of the deaths may not be the work of this killer, and then the subsequent projection of the three floats for the upcoming event.

"The Copenhagen Carnival has had a variety of formats over the years. It's also had bankruptcy and embezzlement in its history. If someone were to be murdered, I think this would be the end of the Carnival," said Nielsen, he then looked over at the FBI. "I judge by your appearance here, that you put weight into the data you've seen so far. You want our help catching your suspect."

"First and foremost, we would like to prevent another death if the Copenhagen Carnival is indeed the target."

"Does this killer favor a particular method for murder? Do we look for someone with a long pipe and a bandoleer filled with darts? Are we looking for a man or a woman? Is the killer American? How do we spot your killer in a projected crowd of 100,000 spectators?"

Natalie felt like she wasn't being taken seriously by the tone of the Constable's statement, so she reminded him, "He or she may also be your killer from another parade. Capturing them would likely solve the murder in Aarhus, or doesn't that matter as it is outside of Copenhagen?"

The second the words were out of her mouth, she worried that she had gone too far. Damn her American arrogance.

"Pardon me, Sir. What you do with your police force doesn't concern me."

There was another silence in the room. Natalie began gathering up her materials, suddenly tired from the excitement of the last few days crashing into the wall of disinterest by this Constable. She covered up a yawn.

"Detective Severino, you are quite right that this might be our killer, and I forgot the case in Aarhus in my rush to solve the mystery of how I will keep 100,000 spectators safe. Tell me more about why you have focused on three of our floats."

"Our computer analyst found your float entries from last year and examined which floats have a costumed character riding on them. It seems that most of the floats have dancers in Caribbean costumes, but these are not the type of costumes that attracts our murderer."

"Is there any pattern as to where in the parade the killer attacks the float? Most parades have routes of one to five kilometers, so do they attack at the beginning or toward the end of the route?"

"Good question. I'll see if I can find that information shortly, I should have thought of that question myself."

Natalie checked her watch, guessing it was still the middle of the night in California. She would send Damian an email in hopes he could answer her question when he woke up. Meanwhile, she would look at the fifteen cases she and her fellow detectives had reviewed, and see if she might determine the answer in that small sample size.

Nielsen looked over at the assembled group and asked, "Any thoughts on how we might find this needle in a haystack? How I might protect the parade participants and spectators, and how we will keep this out of the news?"

Ortiz asked, "Do you have cameras in the area of the parade route? Do you have any details of float entries – sketched pictures? Do you have any blow-up dummies that we might insert inside the costumed characters?"

"Yes, to all of your questions, but what reason do we give the float entry people for not putting one of their volunteers inside a costume?"

"Safety? Someone recently died in the Mardi-Gras parade by falling off the float in New Orleans which is unrelated to our killer, and the parade's insurance carrier wants to make everyone safe?" Ortiz proffered.

"So why then do we allow people to dance on the float?"

"People in costumes have poor peripheral vision, and have accidentally stepped off a moving float."

"That might work. We Danes are much more compliant with regulations than you 'give me liberty or give me death' Americans."

"Good, how deep are spectators along the parade route? Does everyone have a front seat? Is the front row sitting in chairs, and therefore they're lower than a row of people standing behind them upright?" Ortiz continued.

"The parade route goes through crowded downtown commercial areas where people are three or four deep, and then other areas where they're just one deep. The parade is about ninety percent dance troupes. There aren't many floats, and I can't remember seeing more than one or two floats with fully costumed volunteers on them," Nielsen said, looking at his colleagues to see if they had a different experience with the parade.

No one had a different perspective.

"Do you have any other parades with deaths that have so few floats?" asked Nielsen.

"I don't know, Sir, let me find the answer to your question," Natalie said, sending off another email to Damian.

"Perhaps we should take a tour of the parade route, so our American colleagues have a better visualization of where the parade goes and the type of streets here. In my experience, it's vastly different than an American parade route," the Danish Ambassador suggested.

An hour later, they were back at the neoclassical four-story police building. The Danes moved on to planning what they wanted to do. It was relatively simple as they had obtained the float entry list. There were two floats that they had to worry about with a total of three characters in full costume.

The mood in the room was that while everyone believed in the existence of a serial killer, they didn't think that this was the parade the killer would attack. As compared to many parades around the world, it had few floats. If their killer had a float fetish then this parade wasn't for them.

CHAPTER 15

James King was sitting in his penthouse atop the luxury hotel in the nob hill neighborhood of San Francisco. In a city of eccentric people, he was likely the most unconventional of them all. What his neighbors, relatives, friends, and law enforcement didn't know was he had been a killing machine for thirty years. What had started slow, had now snowballed into a biweekly obsession.

At twelve, he wanted to be the tiger character on a float in the San Francisco Chinese New Year parade. That year had been the year of the tiger, and there were many tigers on the floats. His mom put the kibosh on his riding the float in a costume. She said it was for his safety as the float was moving, after all. He found out that the float organizers hadn't wanted him there, and his mother hadn't stood up for him. She let herself be bullied. She didn't stand up for her son.

So he showed them. He studied the float design, and at the age of twelve, he figured out a way to kill the kid taking his place on the float. More importantly, he wasn't caught. There were nearly six years between the first and the second deaths. After a time, he moved it up to an annual killing, then to monthly, and now whenever he felt like it. There was a parade somewhere in the world every week. All it had to have was a fully costumed cat character on a parade float.

His first kill was so easy, the tiger was supposed to lie down like it was taking a nap, while other tigers frolicked around it. It was such a minor character on a float, and yet they couldn't let him be that tiger. He visited the float at the start of the parade. He managed to insert a rag with chloroform under the tiger's head so that he would feel fewer bumps from the street as the float proceeded down the parade route. Nobody recognized the rag was soaked in concentrated chloroform that would cause heartbeat irregularities and result in death. So the tiger died shortly after the start of the parade, but no one noticed the dead costumed child until the end of the parade when everyone got off the float to turn in their costumes. James managed to get close to the float near the end of the parade and remove the cloth, so the coroner assumed the child died from a fatal heart rhythm, but never knew the deadly source of the affliction.

James had a high IQ. School was astonishingly easy for him, which left him time to set traps for his fellow students, just for the fun of watching something bad happen to them. He could study a chemistry textbook and then be able to duplicate the formulation at home. So with his first death, he was able to mix methane and chlorine to get the chloroform that he used to kill his classmate. He tried the concoction out on a few neighborhood animals, which did a great job of killing them.

His next victim died five years later, and again it was a classmate. He attended Sierra Leon Prep school, the home of the wildcats. By the time his graduation ceremony was approaching, he was tired of watching the school mascot get all the attention. He was in the line-up of officials when the students walked on stage to accept their diplomas. The last thing he wanted to do was pose with a mascot holding his diploma, but he found a brilliant smile for the picture. He knew the mascot would be dead before the end of the graduation ceremony. He hugged the mascot and stabbed his neck with the toxin from a pufferfish. He had seen the pufferfish in action in a James Bond film and set up an aquarium in his bedroom. Little did his parents know when he brought home an exotic fish, that he planned to use it to kill another classmate. Of course, they didn't know about the first one. James exited the stage and returned to his seat and watched the remainder of the ceremony. By the time the school reached the last names by the letter R, James had a small smile when the mascot had leaned over to the principal, and likely said that he wasn't feeling well. He took off the head of his mascot costume and moved to sit on a chair toward the back of the stage. He never made it, falling to the floor. The graduation ceremony was abruptly ended, and the remainder of the students were passed their diplomas. A crowd was centered around the mascot, and even one of his fellow student's fathers was doing mouth to mouth resuscitation as they could see he wasn't breathing. Paramedics rushed in, and he was taken off to the hospital with someone bagging him, but James was gleeful when he heard later that evening that the mascot had died in the hospital. His mother looked at him strangely when he failed to display any sadness for his fellow student's death. The police never discovered the toxin in the mascot's blood, and so again, James got away with murder.

James found he liked that science gave him the means to get rid of people he didn't like, so he went to college, where he did a double major in biology and chemistry. By the time he graduated with honors from college, his father had passed away from cancer, and it was just his mother and him. James wondered what he was going to do for the rest of his life. He had his college degree, but he could hardly plan a career in murdering cat costumed parade volunteers.

...Or maybe he could if he could get his mother out of the way of controlling his funds. He had a separate apartment from the house he grew up in, and his mother paid the rent while waiting for James to go to work for a biotech company as befitted his education. Alas, he had no love for his mother at all. She stood in the way of his success. He tolerated that through college, but then decided it was time for her to go away. She had thirty million dollars in the bank, and he was convinced he could turn it into sixty million by buying and trading on Wall Street. Best of all, he would use the money to fly around the world to parades and continue his mission of ending the lives of parade volunteers. He took matters into his own hands and slowly exposed her to a couple of organic compounds to see what would kill her first.

By the time he was twenty-four, he had secured his mother's cash with her early death. He did indeed invest it, and the money grew in size far beyond his mother's initial stake. That allowed him to continue down the path of being a killer of anyone stupid enough to put some kind of cat costume on for a parade float. With each death, he felt like he was avenging his mother and her friend's decision to keep him off the float when he was twelve.

Sometimes, he wondered when he would stop killing people, and he had no answer to that. He supposed it would be when he ran out of parades. He calculated once when he would run out of parades, and the response was sometime in his 90s. When he first started out, he tried a variety of killing methods, excluding knives and guns. Rule number one was don't get caught, and rule number two was confuse the police as to whether it was a homicide or a natural death.

Firing a gun would be loud, and it would violate rule number two. James preferred poisons, gas, and in a few cases, drownings or electrocutions. He tried making someone fall off a float, but they didn't die, and he scratched that off his list as ways to kill. A few weeks ago, he had been in Mexico for the Cinco de Mayo parade and managed to eliminate someone on one of their floats. He took some time before the parade to explore Puebla as the city is famous for its chicken mole dishes. Sometimes it was easy to hide his killing, as the cops were terrible in many parts of the world. When he knew he was facing poor detection, he tried new out new methods. Sometimes he worked on perfecting the latest techniques; other times, he discarded them as unworkable once they failed or created a mess.

He kept a spreadsheet of where he'd been, and where he was going for a year in the future. That way, he didn't visit the same parade twice, and he researched each parade to make sure there were floats with someone wearing a cat costume.

James was forty-five, he'd never married, nor had children. He smiled to himself at that thought. It was probably good that his killing gene hadn't been transferred to another human. He'd dated woman along the way, but it became too much of an effort to hide his spreadsheet and its research. He also hated inventing cover stories for his frequent trips around the world. Really, it was better just to buy sex and forget the more intimate relationships that came with dating women. He was an only child with no siblings to share his parents' fortune, and he hadn't kept in touch with the cousins he'd met in his childhood.

James was a competitive tennis player and played in singles tournaments across the state and nation. He tried doubles, but he didn't like sharing the court with another player, so he was much more suited to singles. He would occasionally socialize with other players when a match was over, but mostly he found his fellow players a bore. Oh well, that was the downside of being so smart, when left to communicate with his fellow humans, he was always disappointed.

The map of the Copenhagen Carnival was spread in front of him. He also watched previous versions of the parade on YouTube. He often, but not always, watched a parade in person to learn how he would approach his kill. The trouble with that kind of research was he had to wait a year for the parade to be hosted again, and the killing urge was overwhelming towards the end of the year's wait.

A few years ago, he'd killed someone from the Aarhus

Christmas parade. After he was done, he went to Copenhagen, and a few other cities to explore future parades. He'd avoided the Copenhagen Carnival as their law enforcement was pretty good. Usually, there was only one float that carried some kind of cat costumed character. The Danes had a cartoon character called the cat queen, or the Kattedroning in their language, that would be his target this year.

The parade traveled some narrow streets, which allowed him to get close. The bigger problem was getting through the thick suit to the parade volunteer underneath. It was a Danish tradition to have a barrel that the cat queen struck as part of the storyline. The barrel would dispense candy to children, and the cat queen knocked the last piece of candy out of the barrel. He thought about poisoning the candy, but he didn't want to kill the attendees, just the cat queen. So he focused on the stick as the costume character had bare hands so they could continue to hit the barrel with the stick. It would have to be a poison on the stick that was absorbed through the skin. He needed the instant gratification of death by the end of the parade, which ruled out plutonium or polonium. Of course, those substances would be tough to obtain. He liked the idea of using fentanyl. He could rub it on the stick, and it should work to bring down the cat queen. First, it would slow down the strikes on the barrel, then the cat would feel drowsy and probably lay down on the float to sleep. Sure, other people on the parade route would notice. Still, unless the cat queen dramatically collapsed, the person driving the float would be busy watching the spectators and would take some time to stop and check on the cat queen. By then, it should be too late.

He tested out his theories at home in San Francisco. He'd purchased sticks the same size that cat queen would use on the float. He then filed down the tip so he could offer the homeless a warm hot-dog on a stick to eat. He then watched as they finished the hot dog, fell asleep, or appeared to be, or might be dead, compared to how he'd applied fentanyl on the stick. Thanks to the few volunteers that had unknowingly given their bodies to his science experiments, he knew how to accurately handle it. He would just switch sticks at the start of the parade, and he should have his death in no more than thirty minutes after the beginning of the parade. With everything thoroughly planned, he left his penthouse for a tennis match.

CHAPTER 16

Shelly Manson and Michael Swatten walked into the offices of BlueSilver to share their findings with the CEO, Fred Rodgers. When the two investigators had taken this assignment, they knew they would be doing a little corporate spying on a small company in Richmond, California, that they had never heard of. There appeared to be less than ten employees, and it inhabited a large three-story warehouse with an excellent restaurant on the first level. They had spent several days in that restaurant learning the lay of the land. The employees often had lunch there, and so they had split up and listened to different conversations. Soon, they discovered that the two youngest members were working on a project that was against the interests of BlueSilver, just as their client, Fred Rodgers, had feared.

One of BlueSilver's technicians had been in a retail store upgrading the beacons and watched the teenagers track the technology. He figured it was for a high school project, but nevertheless, let management know about what he'd observed.

The CEO, just to be safe, had the technician go back to the store and get a copy of the two teenagers' faces from security cameras inside. They had then been able to identify who they were, and through their Instagram page, where they worked. Then, he hired Consolidated Security Systems to find out more about the kids. Even if they were teenagers, he didn't take their effort for granted whatever it was.

Separately, Fred researched Damian's company and had not like what he found. This Damian Green sounded like he was a genius, and Fred was worried that he would be successful in creating an app that would block the beacon signal. There was nothing illegal about the app, and his entire beacon company would go down, as his number one selling product would be rendered useless if everyone began using this new app. He knew that some shoppers would not use the app as they will not have heard of it, or they wanted a particular store's product coupons sent to them by the beacon detection. Still, enough would use it that the company's sales would slump in about six months.

He asked his attorney if he could either sue the kids or the company they work for, but his lawyer hadn't found an angle for that yet. Consumers were entitled to their privacy, and the courts would rule on their side. There wasn't a copyright or patent violation either. If he could change the software of his beacons from Bluetooth to something else like Zigbee, his company would fare well unless the app blocked that as well. He would ask these two private investigators to look into that.

Shelly and Michael were shown into the conference room, and Fred walked in on their heels.

"I read your report about Hermione Knowles and Jacob Moore. I am concerned about the app these two are creating. It sounds like the company they are working for has the technical expertise to be successful. What I want you to do now is some more surveillance on the company."

"Yes, Sir, what specifically are we looking for?" Shelly asked.

"I want to know if this application the teenagers are creating blocks just Bluetooth, or Bluetooth and Zigbee beacons? You're probably not familiar with those terms, but they are both ways for beacons to transmit and communicate with consumer cell phones."

"Yes, Sir, we'll continue to monitor the situation and see what we can find out about the company. We may use some other operatives, as this location is small, and we'll be noticed as unusual visitors soon. However, you'll still get your information."

"Excellent. I look forward to your report," Fred said, as he stood up and left the room, knowing the two investigators knew their way out.

For the rest of the afternoon, he stewed about what this app was going to do to his company. He'd had explosive growth over the past decade as everyone wanted to get on board and track customer behavior in their stores. He kept the company private, resisting the urge to take the company public on the stock exchange. He was his own boss, and he liked it that way. Sure he had advisers, but they were there when he reached out. He considered this the most significant business crisis of his life. He thought about the three-thousand employees he employed around the globe installing his beacons and groaned.

What were his options?

From what he could tell, he didn't have enough money to try and pay off Damian Green, so his company wouldn't build the product.

He needed to annihilate the company before they destroyed him. There was something wrong with the world when a ten-person company could destroy a multi-million dollar company.

The more he thought about it, the more enraged he became, pacing around his office. He had been on the cover of several magazines celebrating his success in business, and now it might be gone within a year.

Maybe the two teenagers would fail...

No, Fred knew when he read the profile of this Damian Green that he didn't fail at things. So even if he eliminated the teenagers, there were plenty of other people at the tech firm that could write the app. It really was a simple solution for consumers, and the more he thought about it, he was surprised that someone hadn't devised an answer to his technology before now.

He needed to end the entire company. Drop a nuclear bomb on the one building when all the staff was inside.

No, that was an outrageous thought. What else could Fred do?

CHAPTER 17

Damian pulled his car to the curb in front of Lily's home the next morning and called her to let them know he was waiting at the curb. Damian looked up and down the street but hadn't noticed anyone following them. Perhaps he was worried about nothing.

"Good morning," Lily and Jacob called out, as they got in the back seat.

"Good morning," Damian and Hermione called back at them.

"Did you have a quiet night?" Damian asked.

"Yes. I've convinced myself that there is no threat to Jacob or Hermione."

"So have I, but I plan an all-staff meeting today, just to hear more voices. The entire company may be at risk as the private investigators don't know who else is working on the app."

"Yeah, I bet these two are back or perhaps someone else from their company. We should take camera shots of everyone that comes to Pete's for the week, and see if they come from this same company," Hermione suggested.

"Maybe we could plant a camera over the door to Pete's and

just use facial-recognition software to identify everyone," Jacob suggested, not to be outdone.

"Wow, you guys sound paranoid. Maybe we should film everyone who enters the street the office is on, or maybe everyone that enters the city of Richmond?" Lily suggested, with sarcasm in her voice.

"We would have to notify everyone that they were being taped on video by California law. If these investigators are any good, they should start coming in disguises so we can't identify them. Any thoughts as to how they found out about you and the project you're working on? Did you discuss it on social media or with your classmates?" Damian asked, knowing the answer was probably no.

"No," chorused Hermione and Jacob together.

"That's what I thought you would say," Damian said, reassuringly. "How about when you were out doing your research on the beacons. Did you notice anyone watching you or listening in on your conversations?"

The two teenagers stared at each other, thinking back to when they surveyed the stores.

"How about when we were in Zellers? Weren't people spying on us there?" Jacob said.

"Yes, but they thought we were planning to steal. Remember, we thought someone was watching us at Caplan's, but when we looked around, we never saw anyone?"

"I remember. It was at Simpson's. There was a maintenance guy in the same aisle as we were," Jacob suggested.

Hermione thought back in her memory and then agreed that the guy watched them.

"He was actually working on the beacons, but he stopped work and listened to us while we were doing our survey. I thought he worked for Simpson's, but he had a blue and silver shirt on, so perhaps he worked for BlueSilver."

"Okay. That sounds like when the cat was let out of the bag, so to speak, and I don't think you could have done anything to stop it. It was just bad luck. Let's go inside and chat with everyone," Damian said as they pulled into the parking lot.

As they got out of the vehicle, they all looked around for someone watching them and saw nothing.

A short time later, after everyone had arrived, Damian called an all-staff meeting. He explained the problem with BlueSilver and his concerns for Hermione and Jacob as well as the rest of the team.

"So they had the sophistication to track Hermione and Jacob here. They have said enough in public to stop store management from arresting them for theft. Still, it was enough through dumb luck to alert a beacon manufacturer. You're concerned for all of us. These two investigators don't know who, if anyone, beyond Hermione and Jacob, is also working on the project. Does that sum up the situation?" Angus asked.

Damian blinked, and replied, "Yes," feeling somewhat chagrined, for worrying over the small problem described by Angus.

"It sounds like the app they are working on would destroy most of the company's revenues, so the real question is how far might a CEO go if his entire company's existence is threatened by a pair of kids. Based on the jerks I met in prison, I would say we're all in danger. If the product was already for sale, I wouldn't worry about it, but if this company goes down in flames, then the Blue-Silver company's future is secured."

Damian felt less paranoid now that Angus had voiced his concerns.

"So, why don't we spy on them?" Haley asked. "What can we learn about them? What if we hack into their computer systems to see what communication is taking place? Don't tell my mother-in-law that I said that. I mean, it's not like someone will show a hitman on their accounting books, but we may still learn something."

Retired Detective Natalie Severino was Haley's mother-in-law.

"Should we have Pete deliver food, so we don't go out at lunch and come and go in pairs?" Chris suggested.

"Maybe I could put a drone above the building to watch 24/7," Haley said.

"Are you going to fly it 24/7 or duck tape the controller, and hope it stays in place?" Damian asked.

"I can put it on auto-pilot."

"But short of watching the video feed real-time, how will you recognize danger or bad people? I don't think we have that programmed yet," Damian said.

"True."

"Okay, why doesn't everyone stay in for meals. We'll have Pete deliver, and we'll regroup at the end of the day to see what everyone has found out about the BlueSilver company."

With that, everyone dropped the projects they were working on and spent the day trying to gain inside access to the BlueSilver company. Damian let his staff try and learn more about the company, while he enhanced the security for the building. It was time to add some unusual defense tactics like he had on his island. Since Damian owned the warehouse, he could install whatever he needed on the roof. He liked Haley's idea of hovering drones, with an ability to drop special dye balloons on someone or pepper juice water balloons. What Damian hadn't figured out was how to make the technology fire on only certain people. Pete would kill him if he started dropping pepper juice on his patrons.

He worked on the safety and security of his employees while they researched the company that was causing their concern. He thought about Ariana's business being firebombed, and could only hope that he wasn't next. His building was off a public street with lower traffic than average, but still, enough that watching the road wouldn't work. Maybe he should ask his employees to work from home, and for all of them to work on the app. Once it was launched, then taking out the company wouldn't do any good. He took a look at his employee homes. He decided he had advice on how they could increase security, but he shouldn't endanger them. He could have everyone work from his island lab. The space was tight for that many people, but they would be safe there. He could set up a boat ride account with the harbormaster to shuttle people there. Yes, he would feel better if he protected his staff that way.

They regrouped later in the afternoon, and Damian started with his own announcement.

"I'm going to put a closed sign on our entrance tonight and maybe a fake 'building for lease' sign as well, so it looks like the company has closed. Tomorrow, if you would all be at the Richmond marina by 8:30, we'll work from my house. I can guarantee your safety there. I looked at adding protection to your homes, and so if you want to hear about that, talk to me after the meeting."

Haley let out a whoop of joy and said, "I will love working from your house. I'll pack some stuff that you can take there tonight, and I'll come with more tomorrow. I have some equipment experiments to run that will be better in the conditions on your island."

Damian was surprised by Haley's comment and said, "While I don't generally like visitors on my island, that's a general attitude, and not a personal one, if you ever need to use it for the weather, wind, or waves, don't hesitate to ask. I would like to add additional minds to the creation of the app because if we launch it, then taking down this company won't make the app go away. Now, what have we found on the company?"

Damian assigned Jacob and Hermione to continue their work on the app, while his other staff researched the BlueSilver company. He admitted to himself that he was curious to see what they had come up with.

"I researched Consolidated Security Systems trying to see if they had been associated with any potential criminal investigations, and by that, I mean, were they associated with any gun violations?" Chris started. "I couldn't find any evidence of any violence on the part of their company. They provide bodyguards and private investigators. I also looked at how many of their operatives in California are licensed for guns. I just checked California as there are different gun laws in different states. About half of their operatives carry guns, but not the two working on this case."

Damian nodded, "That's good information. In theory, Hermione and Jacob are not in any direct danger when around these two investigators."

He made eye contact with Angus, who began a report of his findings.

"So Lily and I studied Fred Rodgers. Since we both spent time around psychotic, manipulative criminals, we concentrated on the smell test to determine if he was like some of the types we met in a previous life."

As both Angus and Lily had done time – Lily for bank robbery and Angus was falsely convicted and released after two decades inside, they had up close and personal experiences with criminals.

"And?"

"We think he is capable of causing great harm to us."

"Why?" asked several voices at once.

"He's a bully that has led a life of privilege. He either bought his competitors or ran them out of business. I looked at how he did it as that says something about the man and his company," Lily said.

Angus continued, "He formed the company out of college. He was a marketing major while his roommate was an engineer. Together they devised the company, but soon after the roommate designed the technology, they had a falling out, and Fred ended up with everything."

"Where's the roommate now?" Damian asked.

"About five years after the two split, he formed his own company that does the same thing with beacons but uses Zigbee instead of Bluetooth. So he's a smaller competitor to Fred on the retail side. Still, he also designs tracking systems for shipping companies. That part of the business is ten times the size of Fred's company, so he came out okay by their split. I don't believe he has a role in our little problem."

"Okay then, back to Fred. He was a low life to what might have been at the time his best friend. What other evidence do you have that he means us harm?"

"He's very greedy," Lily said. "Despite earning millions, he has personally not saved much. He has a loan on his house, cars, and plane. He has two kids in private school. I wonder if he has a drug habit as he's burning through cash. With our technology threatening an already high income that he's barely able to live on, I think his house of cards is about to come crashing down, and Mr. Rodgers has no cushion in his private or business life to soften the blow."

"You're quite the poet with your descriptions," Damian smiled.

"To put it in prison terms, he's waiting to shove a shiv in your back," Angus said.

"Was anyone able to hack into the company's email?" Damian asked.

"I tried," Haley said.

"Tried or succeeded?" Damian asked.

"Succeeded, but I didn't find any useful information. I tried to find certain keywords in his email, but they didn't exist. So either he didn't plan anything nefarious, or Fred deleted that stuff as soon as it was sent."

The conversation continued, and Damian had enough information to worry about, but not enough to take tangible action on. He called an end to the day, and they packed up for their move to his island tomorrow. He dropped Lily and Jacob off at home. Then he and Hermione headed to a big box store to make sure they had enough food and beverages for his staff for the remainder of the week.

CHAPTER 18

Lei Wang worked in the lab of Dr. Cortez as an assistant in the lab. She prepared the agars used to grow the various viruses. She stared at the agars in her hand and felt the beginning of tears running down her face. She didn't want to hurt Viramic as she loved her job, but she also didn't want to hurt her family in southern China. Especially the two young cousins who would be held hostage, if she failed to destroy the agars in the final stages of growth. It would put the company back about three weeks and get her fired. She stood paralyzed with indecision.

Julia happened to be watching Lei's movements because they were not consistent with what she usually saw. The woman was fluid and dedicated. At the moment, though, she was hesitant and jerky. Maybe she wasn't feeling well.

"Lei, are you feeling okay?"

Her employee looked up and into her eyes, and she saw they were filled with tears.

"What's wrong? Did you spill something on yourself?" Julia asked, preparing to come to the woman's aide.

"No," and then suddenly, she was sobbing as tears ran down her face.

Julia repeated, "What's wrong?" as she patted her on the shoulder.

Lei continued to sob, so Julia moved her toward the chair, pushed her into it, and then pulled up another seat and a box of tissues, waiting for the storm to end.

Eventually, Lei looked up and seemed to make a decision.

"I have two young cousins in southern China near the border with North Korea."

Oh no! Julia had a guess as to where this conversation was going. Thanks to the work of Ariana and her friend, she knew what she had to say next.

"You've received word that if you don't destroy the lab work here at Viramic, your young cousins will be harmed," Julia suggested.

Lei looked up and asked, "How did you know?"

"We've had a North Korean company try to hack into our computer systems, and we believe that is who was behind the bombing of our building a few days ago. We figured next that they would go after one of our employees to destroy our work. We just didn't figure out how they would threaten our employees. Are your two cousins in the custody of the North Koreans, or are they with your family in China?"

"They are with my family in China. My family does not know about the threat, either here or in China. I don't know what to do, although I know I can't destroy the experiments since I told you what is going on. So I guess I must get help from law enforcement to save my cousins."

"Let's wait on this a moment. We have an investor on our board who will be really good at finding a solution to keep your cousins safe without harming this company. Are you willing to talk to her?"

"Of course, Dr. Cortez. I'll do anything to keep my job and my family safe."

"I think we can figure out how to do both," Julia said, with more confidence in her voice than she felt at the moment. "Why don't you take a break, maybe wander down to our cafeteria and grab a cup of coffee. I'm going to work on your problem, and hopefully, I'll have an answer for you upon your return."

Lei stood up and shed a few more tears for the kindness exhibited toward her by Dr. Cortez. She should've been mad, but instead, she was trying to help her solve this personal problem. She felt like the luckiest person in Silicon Valley.

Julia looked around the lab to ensure everything was secure, and none of the research was threatened. Then she walked into her office and picked up the phone to call Ariana.

Once she answered, Julia said, "We have a problem. One of my lab assistants, Lei, has family in northeast China. They live across the Yalu River from North Korea."

Ariana interrupted and said, "Your employee's family has been threatened, and you need some help solving this."

Julia gave a sigh of relief at how quick Ariana was to grasp the situation. Not only did she immediately understand the problem, but she didn't panic; instead, she quickly tried to solve it. She and Stefan were lucky to have her as an investor in their Biotech firm.

"Yes, in a nutshell."

"We knew this might happen, which is why we did a background search on your staff. We're lucky your staff member told you about it, rather than threaten the work in your lab."

"So what would you suggest we do next? I sent Lei to the cafeteria for a break, but I could send her home."

"If you can trust her, and I leave that up to you, then I would continue her work as usual. I have some ideas, but let me share them with Damian. In the interim, your employee's relatives aren't in any immediate danger, are they? I suppose we could issue a press release saying that the failure of some of our specimen incubators caused months of research to be destroyed. We would probably bring the FDA or OSHA down on our backs for such a statement. Still, on the other hand, it might give us the time we need to get our patent approved, and then the North Korean bad guys can't threaten Viramic anymore."

"Let me talk your suggestion over with Stefan. We don't want to do anything to jeopardize or slow down our patent approval. On the other hand, if we could figure out what channels of information the North Koreans are watching in the United States, we could put a press release in just that one channel. Regardless, we'll talk it over and call you back."

"Sounds like a plan, we'll talk soon," Ariana said, just before she ended the call.

After Ariana ended the call, she paused a few minutes to think. This attack on Viramic reminded her of the private investigator that went after Hermione. His family was threatened, and she and Damian solved the problem by exposing the person who was doing the threatening. As North Korea was immune to threats from the west for bad behavior, they needed to solve this problem in a different way. Why did North Korea care about her small start-up company? She thought back to the employees, but none of them had Korean ties – north or south. It had to be the product they were working on.

Were the North Koreans trying to steal the technology to sell it themselves?

Ariana thought about that question for a while. She couldn't think of an example of a medical innovation only being sold by North Korea. So it had to be something else and then she thought 'oh my gosh'.

She would bet they were ready to unleash a biological agent on the world that Viramic potentially had the antidote for. She called Julia back.

"Wow, you have an answer already about what to do?"

"No. I've been stuck thinking about motivation. What is the

motivation for the North Koreans to attack your company? The only answer I can think of is they are about to launch a product that Viramic is the antidote for. Could my line of thinking be true?" Ariana asked.

She heard a soft gasp and then silence on the line as the scientist thought about Ariana's line of reasoning.

"They could also be making a product that competes with Viramic, except...." Julia said with her voice trailing off.

"Except that they can't sell on the world market and could care less about patent protection, yes?"

"Yes."

"So, why would they pick a small start-up in California to harass? I think they are planning on unleashing a virus that your solution will counter. It's rather scary, to think about."

Again there was silence on the other end of the phone as a scientist grappled with the idea that North Korea might toss aside their Intercontinental ballistic missiles for an infectious agent that could spread disease around the United States or any other enemy of the state.

"Oh my gosh! What should we do?"

"I'd like to have a few more people confirm my theory before we call the authorities as I'd rather not be labeled a conspiracy theorist. You check with Stefan, and I'll check with Damian, and then we'll go from there. As Stephan is the CEO of the company, likely we would want him to make a call to the FBI or the CDC or the San Jose Police Department. We'll figure out who to call, once we decide it's a good idea to make a phone call and alert people. Do you agree?"

"Yes. Stefan is in the building, so it won't take me a moment to talk it over with him. Why don't you give me a call once you reach Damian and have a discussion with him."

"Sounds good, talk to you soon."

Ariana disconnected one call and was dialing Damian's number a few seconds later. She knew he'd moved his company to his island temporarily. So he was likely at home thinking about providing lunch to his crew.

"Hello, how's your day going?" Ariana asked.

"You know me, I hate to have strangers on my island. My employees are not strangers, but still, I don't like people on my island. They are all as happy as clams. Space is a little tight in the lab, but Haley's been working topside, so it's just the rest of them here. I'm glad I built a second toilet downstairs for Hermione. It's getting a workout with the extra people on the island. What's up with you?"

"If things get really ugly on your island, you could take over part of my house and work from there. It has almost as good protection as your island does. What's more, I have more bathrooms and likely more food in my refrigerator."

She heard Damian chuckle, so she explained the reason for calling.

"The North Koreans made another run at Viramic. One of the employees has had her young cousins threatened by the North Koreans in China unless she destroys the final round of research. Julia was watching her at work today and noticed she was much more erratic than normal. After she broke down and sobbed, Julia heard the story about the cousins. We were discussing our next steps when I got to thinking about motivation."

"Ah," murmured Damian.

"If North Korea is worried about a small microbiology company in California, it must be because that company is developing a product that defeats something the North Koreans consider a weapon. Wouldn't you agree?"

There was silence on the other end, and Ariana knew that Damian's brain was slicing and dicing and putting together data. She imagined a sand timer spinning while his mind considered the options.

"The only other reason I can think of to tamper with Viramic is for malicious mischief, which the North Koreans are known for. However, in this case, I agree the Viramic product, is a threat to something North Korea wants to do. So the question is what you do now with the information you have."

"We have two issues; one, the threat of an infectious agent that North Korea may be planning to launch, and two, how to help Julia's employee's cousins stay safe."

"Yes, you do have the problem with the cousins. I had forgotten about that in the face of what North Korea might do with an infectious agent. For all we know, it may already be released somewhere in the world."

"Yes, we may be in dire straits without knowing it. Julia is talking it over with Stefan. Who do you think we should call? It sounds very far-fetched, and I fear being thought a nut job for trying to explain this problem."

"I may be able to help there. As you know, I'm working on a case with Natalie. The FBI is involved in that case, and I actually met the special Agent in charge two days ago. She tried to hire me, so hopefully, that meeting will open up the conversation between them and Viramic."

"Wow, you'll have to tell me about that meeting sometime. Give me a moment, and I'll check in with Julia and then call you back."

A few minutes later, she reconnected with Damian.

"While I was waiting for your return call, I texted Natalie for the Agent's contact information as she is working with her. She and the Agent are in Copenhagen to catch the parade float serial killer, so she's awaiting my call. I thought I would conference her into this call if that's okay with you?"

"Sounds like the fastest way to gain assistance in this situation. Ultimately, this Agent needs to speak with Julie and Stefan. Still, if we can expedite finding our way through the bureaucracy for Viramic, then that's a good thing."

It was late at night when Natalie notified the agent of another potential issue in her region. Leticia thought it was déjà vu. Just like when she met a certain consulting forensic pathologist for the first time, weird stuff kept coming her way. Now she met Damian Green, and it sounded like he had a strange case he needed help with. Thankfully she wouldn't have to waste time trying to determine if he was legitimate. Her mobile phone rang, and she pushed the connect button.

Damian took a few minutes to describe the situation with the start-up while Ariana explained their virus research. She quickly understood the situation and the two issues at hand. If the theories were correct, Leticia might soon have a massive case of domestic terrorism on her hands. She listened to the story, and then knew she had to get the FBI machinery rolling from nine-thousand miles away. Fortunately, the next day was the parade in Copenhagen. Their killer would be taken into custody, charged with murder around the world, or Damian's projection was wrong and she would head home, embarrassed for contacting the Copenhagen Police. Meanwhile, there was something big happening at home. With instructions to her assistant agent in charge, she tried to get some sleep. It was exhausting covering all the time zones.

The next morning, she was grateful for the organization of the Danes. She and Natalie were retrieved from their hotel with their luggage as they would be going home even if the float killer was located. The killer would stand trial in multiple countries. The FBI agent assigned to Copenhagen could take over the operation. Mostly she was just curious to see if the killer would show up. Leticia was convinced since they had the support of local law enforcement, that if this parade was the target, the killer would be in custody by the end of the parade.

The police made arrangements to place their own personnel on the three floats with costumed characters. Besides the full coverage costume, they also had body armor and were fitted with a microphone. They would be doing one-minute check-ins with a nearby support van. Leticia was impressed with what the Danish Police had arranged on short notice.

The floats were toward the back of the parade, and so Leticia and Natalie watched many dance troupes moving to the music of the Caribbean - Samba, mambo, and others. The women were scantily clad in some of the troupes. Natalie let herself lose her concentration at the beginning, but pretty soon, she was back in cop mode watching the parade spectators. She realized that she couldn't tell who might be their killer as this was Scandinavia and she wasn't used to the customs here. People that appeared suspicious might be exhibiting a custom foreign to her. They stayed toward the back of the parade, planning on walking beside the first float as it made its way.

Leticia had an earbud connecting her to the command center, but she didn't understand their language. She could recognize the various call-ins from the floats, but they could have said they were on fire, and the agent wouldn't have understood. Natalie was holding a camera, filming everyone, and could see the float was finally in motion. They had been standing there an hour before they saw something tall moving and knew it was the float. Again the routine call-ins were continuing.

There was a change in the cadence of the voices as the float got close to them. And then the float came to a halt, and there were many emergency responders approaching the float. She noticed that the cat queen was lying down, not moving, having dropped the stick he had been using to strike the barrel.

Leticia and Natalie approached the police leader to find out what was happening.

"What's going on? I was listening to check-in, but I don't speak your language."

"Officer Agard said he was feeling faint, and then he stopped responding and collapsed. He's not breathing, but his heart hasn't stopped. We're treating him, and we'll get him to the hospital."

"Any sign of what caused the collapse?" Agent Ortiz asked. She supposed someone could pass out from the heat inside the costume.

"Not yet. He's unconscious, so we'll see what the problem is at the hospital."

Leticia watched as they cut away the man's costume in their rush to save him.

"You should bag the costume and everything on the float immediately so your crime scene folks can examine stuff," Agent Ortiz suggested, nervous about the crowd, and someone moving evidence off the float.

"Good point. If I wasn't so concerned about my officer, I would have thought to do that."

He said something over his microphone, and immediately the cops moved everyone away from the float. An ambulance backed in and whisked the officer away. Leticia looked around at the crowds but had no idea who their killer might be. Natalie was still filming the scene.

"Did you see anything suspicious?" Leticia asked Natalie.

She shook her head and said, "They all look weird to me. What happened to our costumed character?"

"He's on his way to the hospital, not breathing, but otherwise in good shape. Thankfully, they thought of those one-minute check-ins, or he might have been dead by the time someone noticed he was down."

The two women looked over at the float as another commotion occurred. Natalie saw another officer pass out as she was trying to collect evidence off the float. Fortunately, there were other people nearby.

She looked at the scene a moment longer than went back to the Copenhagen police leader and said, "It's the stick. Someone put something on the stick that is causing people to pass out. You need to instruct your staff to wear a mask and handle it with caution, and get it immediately to your crime lab."

Again, the leader said something over his microphone, and she watched as her suggestions were followed through.

"My apologies, Sir, I don't mean to instruct you or your officers," she said in apology.

"I appreciate your instincts, I'm a little slow today as I thought this was just a crazy idea from the Americans as it was so far-fetched. Instead, you've been spot on. Did you see a suspect?"

"Unfortunately, no. We recorded the parade, but the stick must have been placed on the float close to the start of the parade. Do you have any cameras in that part of the town?"

"We do. Let's hope we have one in the right place. We have some more cleanup here with the crime scene, but Constable Nielsen has called a meeting at headquarters in thirty minutes. Please stay close to me so I can transport you there."

"Okay," responded the agent. She waved Natalie over, and the two of them moved within the vision of the Danish officer, but not within hearing distance. She didn't want to interfere with his communication with his officers.

"We're heading to their headquarters for a meeting in thirty minutes. Then we'll be heading back to San Francisco this afternoon. Your friend Damian has an even more pressing issue than this."

"I know. Infectious agents are scary. Is your office working on that?"

"They are. By the time we return, another group from Quantico, the CIA, and the CDC will be in San Jose. They should be able to establish a credible threat by the time we arrive. You're having a quiet retirement, aren't you," Leticia said, energized by the two cases.

"These cold cases have been far more intriguing and dangerous than I ever expected. I wished I'd worked on a few while I was an active detective. I have to say though, that you are working at warp speed."

"Wouldn't have it any other way," Leticia said, with a smile.

They continued watching the action for a while. Then they got the nod to accompany the officer to a car, and shortly they were at the white neoclassical government looking building.

They walked into the conference room behind the other officer. They found people on their laptops and Constable Nielsen at the head of the table.

"Our officer is recovering, he's regained consciousness, and should be released from the hospital later today if we identify the substance on the stick. Thank you, Special Agent Ortiz, from stopping more of my officers from being exposed."

"You're welcome, Sir. Do we have any video of the suspect?" Ortiz asked, looking over at the people on the laptops.

"We should have something. One of our traffic cameras was aimed at the float. We have our technicians going through the footage to locate someone placing a stick on the float. Liam, why don't you hook your computer up to the projector and we can all watch as you look at the video footage?"

The technician did as ordered and soon they were all looking at the footage. They saw the float being pushed into place about two hours before the parade started.

"Can you freeze the video and focus on the stick used by the cat queen? Does the stick come with the barrel, or does it come with the cat queen costume?" Ortiz asked.

Initially, her Danish colleagues looked blankly at her, but then they understood her question.

"I don't know if anyone in this room has rented a cat queen costume to know the answer to your question, Special Agent," Nielsen replied.

Meanwhile, the technician named Liam focused on the stick sitting on the float. They could see the stick sitting in a clear plastic bag underneath the barrel.

"Is that the original stick or the one used by your officer?" Ortiz asked.

"I don't know" was the consensus by everyone in the room.

"Okay, let's continue the video feed now until the time that our officer gets on the float."

The video moved forward at a speed slightly faster than usual. They saw a group of people approach the float and reach for something on the float. That appeared to be their officers reaching for the costumes to put on over their street clothes. There was conversation and laughter, but as far as Leticia could see, no one got near the stick, and it was nearing the time the float was about to move for the first time. Then she saw it.

"Wait, freeze the video," she exclaimed. Then she stood up and approached the screen and pointed.

About twenty feet in front of the float just on the edge of the screen was a man carrying a clear plastic bag with a stick in it.

The technician put the video feed in reverse at about half speed, and the room was silent as all eyes were on the man rather than the float.

"Our killer is a 'he', and he certainly does his homework. He knew when the overhead camera would be blocked from seeing the stick and had perfect timing to affect the change," Ortiz said. "Now, are there any videos featuring his face where we could identify him?"

"We need to put our borders on alert, so our suspect doesn't get out of Denmark."

"Short of stopping all male traffic from leaving the country, I'm not sure we have enough of a description to do any good at stopping him at the border," said someone else in the room while everyone's eyes were focused on the screen looking for a view of their killer.

"Someone might want to look in the trashcans lining the parade route to find the stick he's carrying. Perhaps he will have left some DNA on the bag even though his hands appear to be gloved," Natalie suggested.

The officer in charge of the scene nodded and stepped away to have a search done. No one knew if that search would be successful, given that their suspect could dump the stick anywhere. The stick might be covered with food detritus to the exclusion of any DNA.

Leticia had been keeping an eye on the clock, not wanting to miss their flight back to the U.S. She did a quick scan of what she knew about this case and what the Danish police were in the process of doing. They would stay on the case as one of their officers had been hurt and could have died. She stood up after whispering to Natalie that it was time to leave.

"I can tell this case is in good hands here in Denmark. Natalie and I will catch a taxi to the airport as we have trouble brewing back in San Francisco. Please email any information you have on our suspect – the best picture you can get of his face and any other estimates like height, weight, or age. Keep me posted on what your crime lab finds as well. I'm going to go back to my civilian expert to see if we can get another estimate of where he will strike next. My colleague here in Copenhagen will stay as deeply involved in your case as you allow her. We'll continue to funnel any new information we gain. Is that acceptable to you, Constable?"

"Yes, Special Agent Ortiz. We appreciate your help on many levels. We would have likely had a homicide on our hands today. It would have been the death of one of our citizens and subsequently the Copenhagen Carnival. Instead, your actions saved both. Thank you."

Leticia thought about saying more, but just nodded and headed for the door, wheeling her carry-on case.

She missed the gestures Constable Nielsen made behind her back, but soon found that she and Natalie had a police escort to the gate. She was pleased to see the sign for San Francisco, and boarding had begun.

CHAPTER 20

James King was enjoying Copenhagen. He'd been there for two days and was impressed with the food, museums, and weather. Apparently, the other Danes were as well as they were out in droves. There were a few events leading up to the parade that he visited. While he liked the scantily clad women, he found the Caribbean theme a bore. He had been to other Caribbean events in other cities that did the theme better. Still, he guessed he could understand the desire to think of the Caribbean after the long cold winter in Denmark.

He knew where the parade started and how everyone lined up to begin. There was a float at the start, and the two floats he was focused on at the end. He figured he could mix with the crowd and exchange sticks. He saw the float from past parades and knew how to make a trade of the sticks used to strike the barrel. His other purpose was to study where the cameras were around town. He'd been killing people a long time and hadn't been caught. He liked to think that was because he spread his talents out across the globe, and he was careful in planning and execution. He planned like the authorities were aware of his activities, and wanted to capture him.

He wore a variety of disguises when he was near the parade route so that he still couldn't be identified if he made a mistake and was caught on camera. He also studied the parade exit routes in case he needed to run. He usually had two ways away from a parade, and he had never had to use those routes. Once or twice he'd been careless, and had no escape plan. Still, he didn't like the feeling of an incompletely executed murder. Some of his joy in killing came from having every detail perfect, and death was proof of his genius.

It was the morning of the parade, and he dressed with disguise in mind. He had a coat that was reversible that he would take off and change the color of after he dropped off his murder weapon – a stick in this case. He kept three hats - a knit cap, a baseball cap, and a beret. All were different colors. He also had a gaiter that he could pull up and down as suited him. He carried several pairs of sunglasses, all designed to block his eyes and distort the light hitting his cheeks, which confused any facial identity software.

With the overhead camera in mind, he waited until the parade volunteers had their backs to the float to make his exchange. He'd studied magic with a magician in Las Vegas so he could learn to move his hand with someone not noticing. James incorporated that training here. His hand moved quickly to make the change. He was glad the stick had come in a clear plastic bag as that allowed him to contain the dispersal of the fentanyl. People would probably pass out near the float if the stick was out in the open.

The night before he'd looked for a place to discard the stick, and he discovered a cabinet maker down a small alley off the parade route. He made a quick detour to dump the original stick in their large trash bin as it wouldn't look out of place therein. He quickly returned to the parade street as he didn't want to miss his dead characters go by on the float. That was a part of the thrill of the killing; to see a float pass him with a dead body on board.

He took a moment to watch the dance troupe in front of him, and then looked back down the street to where the float had been.

There seemed to be a commotion, but there were too many people in his way to see what was going on. Maybe the float had mechanical problems, and they were awaiting a tow truck. That happened more often than anyone realized. He could tell any parade organizer that they should prepare to have at least one float breakdown.

He moved closer to the crowd to see what was going on and was startled to see the cat queen under the care of paramedics. They had a mask over his face and were ventilating what appeared to be a man under the costumed head.

Drat!

He must have called out before the fentanyl overcame him. So, he probably wouldn't die.

Double drat!

He had occasional failures, but those were less than once a year. He would have to eliminate this method from his murder method list as it seemed to give someone the ability to call out for help rather than dying quietly. He watched a while longer and noticed a lot of law enforcement types helping the stricken man. He moved a step close as though walking away from the parade and saw that the man's body armor had been loosened. What was he doing wearing that under a cat queen costume?

Then he began to panic. Were the police on to him? He quickly made his way away from the parade and back to his hotel. He stopped a few times along the way in a doorway or other secluded space to do quick apparel changes. He reached his hotel and changed into a business suit, checked out, and was on his way to the airport for his private jet to take him back to California. He could monitor the situation on the ground in Copenhagen through an internet connection in his plane. He heaved a sigh of relief when he was in the air.

Maybe the cops were a last-minute substitute as part of a charity thing or something. While he'd walked through the area, they hadn't seemed to be acting like it was a crime scene, but who knew what happened after he left.

He read the press release online in the Copenhagen Times as he was descending into San Francisco. It said an officer had been injured in a volunteer activity the day before. He was doing well and would be back on the job. No mention that they were looking for a murderer.

James smiled; his crusade to kill costumed cats on parade floats continued. On to planning his next kill in Tel Aviv, Israel. In the middle of June, Israel hosted a children's start of summer celebration that filled the streets with floats. In examining pictures of past years, he was sure he would find a float with the a cat aboard it. He just needed to study the parade pictures to find his target.

CHAPTER 21

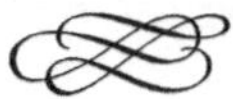

Special Agent in Charge Leticia Ortiz landed at San Francisco International airport exhausted after a twelve-hour flight across too many time zones. She got some sleep, but she was really excited about both cases, and neither was solved.

She and Natalie parted ways. Natalie was headed home with her husband, while Leticia was headed to the Palo Alto office to meet with Viramic and many other folks. An agent drove her the fifteen miles to the meeting location, and she saw she was the last to arrive. The Assistant Agent in Charge was performing introductions when Leticia walked in.

"Sorry I'm late folks, I'm Leticia Ortiz, Special Agent in Charge of the FBI San Francisco office. I seem to have two large, complicated cases on my hands. Has everyone been introduced?"

She looked around at nods and then approached the people she didn't know – these must be the Viramic people. She looked for Damian Green and didn't see him.

"Where's Damian Green?"

Ariana sighed, not liking to bring personal information into this forum, but she couldn't think of what else to say.

"Damian and I share the raising of a teenager. That teenager is working for Damian's company on a project. We're not sure if she's being threatened or just watched by another company, so we don't want to leave her alone at the moment even though she's sixteen."

"He seems to have his hands in many complicated situations at the moment. I'll call him after the meeting as I have questions for him."

"He said he's available to meet you tomorrow if you can get transportation out to his island as he has his company working from there this week given the potential danger the company faces," Ariana just hated explaining, and everyone was looking at her wide-eyed.

"Okay, back to the situation at hand. I understand that you've had several threats hit Viramic over the last two weeks. The most recent was a threat made to an employee. We don't have a bombing suspect yet for the firebombs thrown at your building. Damian Green was able to trace someone trying to hack your computers back to North Korea. So you have one employee issue to solve and a potential major issue for the United States, given what your company makes. Do I have that correct?"

Leticia felt a little fuzz-brained from all the travel in the last two days, and both cases were using up stores of adrenaline. Still, she checked in with her people to make sure that what she said was correct.

She looked around the room for agreement, and she got nods.

"Let's solve the employee problem first. Can the CIA influence the Chinese government to protect the two young cousins of the Viramic employee?"

"Now that we understand what our role might be here, we'll get to work on that," said the CIA representative.

"Keep in mind that you're also involved in the second half of the equation. We need some intelligence out of North Korea to confirm our suspicions. I mean, this is a huge issue, if it is true."

The CIA representative nodded, acknowledging it was a huge problem.

"Okay, perhaps the Viramic people can explain their technology to me. I think I understand it, but it never hurts to confirm it."

Julia nodded and began, "Our world is filled with agents that are infectious to humans. Many we have seen before, and we have solutions for those infections. However, increasingly, mankind is spending time close to wild animals, and those animals contain their own viruses that humans have never been exposed to before. That makes them very dangerous to us, for we have no solutions for treatment and prevention. What Viramic has come up with is a ready for production vaccine that can counter any infectious agent. We do that in two ways. We block the infection's genetic material from replicating. We also duplicate the sterile non-replicating genetic material so that a human also forms the antibodies for this foreign agent. We thought the technology would be used in Africa as that continent has seen a rash of strange infections recently mostly coming from monkeys. It could also be used to treat influenza. We will put it into production as soon as the FDA approves."

The FDA representative followed Julia's explanation with, "Yes, we're reviewing your data, but we didn't fast track it as we're not in flu season, and it seemed to have no other use inside the U.S. I will change that tonight. The North Koreans would be unable to sell the technology to the rest of the world. So I think what you all fear, is the North Koreans are worrying about the technology as it might stop something they're planning. Is that correct?"

There was grim silence with that pronouncement, then Special Agent Ortiz said, "I believe that is why we are all gathered in this conference room."

"So the North Koreans don't have a precise handle of where your technology is as far as being ready to go to market. Correct?" asked the CIA.

"Yes, that appears to be the case. We are doing other research, but the survival of the company is not dependent on that. Rather, it's the scientific evidence in front of the FDA at the moment. That technology, pending FDA approval, will drive our revenues for the future," Julia replied.

"I'm going to say what everyone is thinking. Viramic is ready to ramp up vaccine production should the North Koreans unleash a new virus on the United States," Ariana said. "Isn't this the reason, the only reason they would have a focus on such a small American company? Who here has another theory?"

"Maybe this is just the North Koreans messing with the rest of the world as they're prone to do," said the CIA.

"Certainly releasing an infection that the world has not seen before would 'mess with the world'," Ariana said with sarcasm loaded in her voice.

"We really need some foreign intelligence here. If we have a virus that may already be circulating in the United States, how do we know that? How can we find out if the North Koreans have a lab to create such a virus? We will want to take some big steps tonight if this is a credible threat. We would need to close our borders and ramp up the production of the technology in this company. Of course, Dr. Cortez, from what I understood of your explanation, you need a verified case of the infection to it extract its DNA, correct?" Ortiz said.

All eyes were on Julia, waiting for an answer.

"Yes, that's correct. I would need a few days in the lab to replicate it, and then we could go into production. We could have the first vaccine available a week later. It would be helpful to know if the North Koreans have created a new bacteria or new virus, as the answer to that question will play into my timeline."

Agent Ortiz looked at her watch, which had, fortunately, reset itself as she traveled through the time zones.

"It's almost ten o'clock at night and nearing one in the morning in Washington DC. I think we're all going to have to roust our people out of bed to determine if we have a credible threat coming from the North Koreans. The FDA needs to complete its review to decide if we have a solution in the technology created by Viramic. Those involved in the review process need to be brought into the office now. We all have bosses that we need to notify about our pursuit of this problem. Depending on what we find, I suspect this group's leadership will transfer from me to someone higher up. Still, in the interim, I'm going to run down this problem as I've been trained to do. I'm going to move our meeting to our San Francisco office as it has more space, computers, and secure telephone lines than this location.

"Dr. Cortez, Mr. Weiss, Ms. Knowles, I would suggest you go home, but stay available by phone. For the staff, who flew in from Washington, let's move you to the San Francisco offices. At this time of night, it will be about a twenty-five-minute drive. I think we'll be working all night and there are shower and food facilities in the building. Did I leave anything out? Does anyone have a better plan?"

"This question is for the FDA - do you want us to begin research on who we can contract with to make the vaccine in this area, or do you already have your own contacts?" Julia asked.

"We need absolute discretion on the situation," Agent Ortiz said. "While the question you're asking is important, we can't afford to cause a global panic with unconfirmed information. I pledge everyone to silence. You should have no communication with your family about this issue. We don't want to be responsible for a stock market crash tomorrow morning. I'm going to ask that each of you give me a nod that you understand the catastrophic ramifications of telling anyone outside of this room of our potential problem with North Korea."

Shortly there was silence in the room as she had each person give their solemn nod. The meeting broke up with everyone reaching for their cellphones to gather information for the ongoing operation as they made to leave the building.

Ariana briefly spoke with Julia and Stefan in the parking lot before leaving.

"When I joined your company as an investor, I never dreamed we would reach this stage. I have a feeling Viramic is going to hit the big stage in the next few days, as I do think we have a credible threat coming from North Korea."

"Yeah, I went from thinking I had a more efficient way to make vaccines to potentially being the savior of the west if the FDA validates my methods," Julia said.

"Oh, I think we'll be getting approval tomorrow," Stefan said with confidence. "You did excellent work, and our application was thorough, and the research was excellent and proved our technology. I'll do the dishes for the next six months if I'm wrong."

Both Ariana and Julia laughed at his bet and said goodbye heading to their respective cars.

Once Ariana hit the freeway, she called Damian.

When he answered, she said, "Agent Ortiz is probably going to call you and make arrangements to visit you, and perhaps try to consume your time."

"She's already tried that," Damian replied with a sigh.

Ariana chuckled, "I think she's impressed that not only do you have involvement in Natalie's cold case, but you've touched Viramic. You saw trouble coming, and now you have the potential problem with BlueSilver. Did she make arrangements to visit you on the island tomorrow?"

"In not so many words, I've been ordered as a matter of national security to FBI headquarters in San Francisco with my most powerful laptop in hand. I don't like leaving Hermione alone on the island even though she knows how to defend it. Is there any chance you could work from here?"

"I'm not required to be physically anywhere tomorrow. So I'll reach your dock at seven. Will that give you time to get across the Bay for your meeting with the agent?"

"Yeah. Special Agent Ortiz was so insistent that she was going to send a helicopter to fetch me. I talked her out of that with the promise of showing up to her building by eight. So I'll have my speed boat ready to go."

"Okay. I'll bring food and beverages with me for your staff, so you don't have to worry about them."

"Thanks, Ariana. I would say come over tonight, but it's already late, and crossing the Bay at midnight would leave me too worried to get any sleep. I have a feeling I'm going to need it for the days ahead. Natalie hasn't called me this evening. I know she's going to ask for my computer to do another run on where the next predicted murder will take place. Fortunately, since this killer spaces out his activities by at least three weeks, I've got a few days before I have to do that computer work."

They ended the call, and Damian headed to bed hopeful of getting some sleep before his early boat ride across the Bay.

CHAPTER 22

Natalie Severino realized she wasn't getting any younger when after her husband picked her up at the airport, she fell asleep on the way home. She woke up long enough to walk into their house and change out of her travel clothes before she sunk into a deep sleep, happy to be in her own bed after a whirlwind couple of days.

She woke up refreshed the next morning and ready to work on the case. She'd kept her Lieutenant and Captain informed on her activity in Washington and Copenhagen. She also received additional information from the Danes, and now she had more data to enter into her murder binder. She knew that Agent Ortiz had another big problem and that Damian was involved in it. She would wait a few days before asking for his help.

First, she wanted to do a deep dive into the cases they had already. She planned to look in detail at the methods the killer chose, the demographics of the victims, and placement of the floats in the parades. She also wanted to take another look at the costumes. They thought he only chose float riders in full costume, but she wanted to verify that. She sat down at her home office and went to work. She started by re-reading the original fifteen cases that her colleagues had researched.

She pulled out a poster board and began collecting data in as much detail as she could find. Where the details were missing from the police reports, she searched for newspaper articles that might carry more information about the 'accidents'. While they had cases from around the world, she kept her research to English speaking locations. She would hate to lose critical data by using an online translation software that misstated the facts of a case.

She spent the entire day on her chart, blown away by the heartbreaking data she was looking at. Children as young as five and grandparents in their seventies had all died by this killer. What was even sadder was many of the parades never again took place. Natalie didn't know if the parade organizers couldn't over-come the liability or the sadness related to the volunteer's death. However, in each case, the entire town took a hit from that one parade float death.

When she finished looking at one-hundred-fifty odd cold cases, she smiled. She had a new data point. The cases all had something in common. The person murdered was in some form of a cat costume. There were lions, tigers, cats, and leopards, and cartoon cats like Figaro, Garfield, and Felix. Now she understood why the cat queen was attacked on the float in Copenhagen. Knowing this would allow law enforcement to pinpoint not only the parade but the float.

Natalie picked up her phone, while at the same time debating who to call. Damian would be proud of her as it was a piece of data his big ass computers hadn't discovered. She should also call her Lieutenant and Special Agent Ortiz. Natalie should clarify with her department who would be talking with the FBI. In the end, she dialed the Lieutenant's number. She may as well start there.

"Natalie, how was your star-studded last few days?" asked the Lieutenant.

"I'm glad I retired when I did. I don't have the energy to go gallivanting around the world and then back again in a blink of an eye. The Copenhagen police were quite accommodating. As you can imagine, they were trying to be nice to us while we were on a wild goose chase. Then when one of their officers was stricken by a substance on the cat queen's stick, we suddenly looked legitimate."

"Okay, that's a new term. What's a cat queen?"

"It's a Danish story told to children. The cat queen carries a stick and strikes the barrel, and then candy falls out. Remember, this is the land of Hans Christian Anderson and all of his fairy stories."

"But you were unable to catch our suspect, let alone identify him, right?"

"Unfortunately, that's true. We did identify him as a male, and the Danes gave us a good estimate of height and weight, but that's not enough to search for him at all. However, Lieu, I'm calling to share a new discovery with you. I figured out who his target is in a parade. He only kills lions, tigers, cats, leopards. That's great news because we can eliminate cases where the person that died during the parade was not costumed as something from the cat family. If we narrow his targets, it will make the next parade easier to set up an operation for. The Copenhagen Carnival only had three floats, but can you imagine if the computer said the Rose Parade was the next target? That would have been a nightmare to figure out."

"That's good news, Natalie, and you're correct that it makes the next operation we have to catch this guy easier. Who else have you shared that with?"

"Just you, Lieu. I've done a spreadsheet that describes our victims in details that I'll send to you. But how do you want communication to go? Do you or the Chief want to relay information to the FBI and the Copenhagen Police? Do you want me to do that? This cold case exploded before I had the chance to clarify that with you."

"My instinct is to have you be our point of communication with a copy to me on all communications. This is a cold case that we're trying to solve, not an ongoing incident. That's not to say it's not important, but at this point, you don't need the resources of the SJPD. Special Agent Ortiz has a good reputation, she won't look to blame you for any failed operations. But I better run that by the chain of command and get back to you. Is there anything else I need to know?"

Natalie thought about what she knew about the Viramic case but decided to stay silent. She knew enough to be worried, but not enough to explain it to her Lieutenant, so she remained silent.

"That's it, Sir."

"Congrats on the cat thing as that will help narrow the chase to catch this guy. I'll call you back shortly on what to do about the lines of communication."

They ended their call, and Natalie stretched back in her chair. She'd done a lot of sitting in recent days. She was grateful that she had to stand at the parade yesterday. Maybe tomorrow, she would make it to the gym to undo some of the damage she caused by all the recent sitting.

An hour later, the Lieutenant got back to her as promised. The communication would go just as he suggested. However, she was to personally call command of the perp's identity or his capture.

Natalie stood up and did a little happy dance. Then she sat back down and called Special Agent Ortiz. Her call was answered on the third ring, and the agent clearly had Natalie's phone number plugged into her phone as she said, "Hi Natalie. What's up?"

"I made another discovery about our parade float killer, and I wanted to share that with you in case your technical people could do anything with the information. The killer only targets charac-ters wearing some type of cat costume."

"What!" exclaimed the agent?

"Yes, I spent the day going over in detail what happened in each float death. Do you know he killed people from age five to seventy-three? Anyways, I concentrated on the police reports for float deaths that were completed in English as I didn't want to misinterpret because of translation issues. All of the victims he's killed have been lions, tigers, or cats. Some variation of a costumed cat character has been killed in each float death."

"Wow, that's significant. I wonder what our behavior analysis unit will make of that detail? Certainly, this makes it easier to capture him at the next parade if we have good intel on where the cat characters are in the parade route."

"Yes, I was going to call Damian and ask him to rerun his data for the next projected hit with the cat character in mind. Maybe we'll have greater faith with his computer's guess if we know there's a cat on a float somewhere in that parade."

"He's here with me, I'll pass it on to him. He may be a few days doing your data."

"I figured he would be tied up with your project for a few days. As our killer strikes no sooner than three weeks apart, we have some time to figure out the next city. Since Damian was accurate on the last guess, let's hope he's spot on the next parade."

"Keep me posted, Natalie."

"Will do."

After they ended the call, Natalie gave thought to Damian spending the day in Special Agent in Charge Ortiz's company. She bet by this time of day, Damian would be starting to dislike the FBI. However, he would tolerate their crap and then throw up force fields to surround his island and himself so he couldn't be bothered with them again. With that thought, she switched gears and wondered what she was going to cook her husband for dinner.

CHAPTER 23

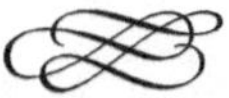

Damian arrived at the appointed time to the government looking building in the civic center district of San Francisco. It had been a foggy and wet drive across the Bay in his little speed boat. He docked it at one of the yacht clubs around the Bay and caught a ride-share service car to the civic center.

He wondered what the Special Agent wanted him to do. It was a shame that she specifically asked that he bring his laptop. Otherwise, he could've listened to a request, and gone back home to do whatever kind of data run she wanted. He had a feeling that she or other FBI people might be looking over his shoulder as he obtained data for them. That would generally be a problem for him as he often used illegal methods to collect cyber information. However, in this case, he was reasonably sure he was going to be asked to hack into North Korea, and there was nothing illegal about doing that.

After going through a security check, he was escorted to a conference room by someone from her office. He looked around the room, assessing what everyone was doing and what he might be called upon to do. People had the look of little sleep and too much caffeine. They were in small groups huddled in conversation. Agent Ortiz looked up and nodded at him when he arrived but finished the conversation she was in the midst of. Great, thought Damian, she's going to waste my time. Then he felt the air change behind him as someone else entered the room. He stepped aside, judging where he should sit, so he could make a quick and silent exit.

Again, Agent Ortiz looked up at the newcomer, and this time gave the new arrival her full attention. Ah, thought Damian, this is who the agent was waiting for. He looked over his shoulder to see if he could deduct what agency this person represented. He then did a double-take as he recognized the person as the Director of the FBI. Oh my, she brought in the big guns over the issue Ariana's start-up was having. This might get interesting. Maybe he would make a friend for future help if he needed it one day.

With the arrival of this VIP, Special Agent Ortiz stood up, ready to command the room's attention. Damian sat close to the doorway, still with a plan to disappear when he had the chance.

"We have some new arrivals that I would like to introduce to everyone," after she confirmed the man he thought to be the FBI Director, Damian listened as she introduced several other agencies. He decided he was impressed as he believed she had the right people in the room. She had been able to do that while chasing down a serial killer in Copenhagen.

The agent gave a quick overview of what had happened up to the point when Ariana left the meeting last night. Then she discussed the information that people in the room had worked on overnight.

"We've spent the night trying to verify or deny that North Korea might have developed an infectious agent not seen by the West. That would, of course, do great damage to the population as we wouldn't have a vaccine or a treatment for the agent. As of this moment, we've been unable to get confirmation one way or another of the existence of this mystery agent."

"And the two children at risk in eastern China, has the CIA secured their safety?" Damian asked as Ariana had asked him to keep the lives of the two children in front of people.

Someone else in the room spoke up and said, "The children have been secured. We have let the Viramic CEO know that the children are safe, and so I believe we can take that off the table as a problem to be solved."

"Excellent," responded Damian, texting Ariana to let her know.

A few other reports were stated, but nothing that really added to the information in the room. The FDA thought it would approve the Viramic product by the end of the day at the latest. So Damian guessed he was going to be asked to hack into North Korea to find out what they were up to. This presented quite a problem to him, as he didn't understand the Korean language. Furthermore, there were smart minds in this room, and they hadn't succeeded in confirming the rumors. How could he search North Korea differently to get an impression about the state of their infectious agent? He decided to see if there was an outflow of additional people from North Korea as surely any viral scheme to infect people would require additional people to arrive in the United States from North Korea. He opened his laptop and began to type. A few minutes later, he had his answer.

Damian had tuned out the conversation while he had his computer fetch data for him. Now, he started to listen again and found a moment to cut in.

"I just did a check of the North Koreans entering the United States, Canada, and Mexico, and there's been a ten-fold increase in the past week. Granted, there aren't many travelers, so it doesn't take much to get that kind of increase. Wouldn't that put validation in the theory that North Korea was up to something?"

All eyes turned toward Damian, and he patiently waited for someone to ask him a question. Finally, one of the engineers in the room that had been doing quite a bit of typing on his own laptop popped his head up and asked, "How do you know that? We haven't got a report from Homeland Security."

"Okay. Well, when you get the report, it will say that traffic is up by ten times the normal rate of traffic."

Damian thought he had to quickly get out of this room, or he was going to become a rude twit.

"Mr. Green, that was exactly why I requested that you attend this meeting. You seem to be faster than anyone else in thinking of needed data and going out and grabbing it. I'm sure you're correct about the ten-fold increase, which would be a clear signal that something is underway," Agent Ortiz said.

"Would you like a list of passenger manifests for the planes they arrived on to the United States, Canada, and Mexico? It was already a part of my search, so I can email it to someone in this room."

A few people had their hands up, and Damian sent the list. If the passengers were exposed then by the North Korean agents, it was helpful to have a contact list to trace additional infections.

"Mr. Green, do you have any ideas on how to confirm what is happening with this increase in visitors?"

Damian had been thinking about just that and had an idea.

"How about if we reach back to the company that originally tried to hack into Viramic. It was called Naegohyang. It manufactures a variety of products, none related to anything close to infections. If we could do an analysis of who is going in and out of their building that might give us a clue. Don't you have spy satellites focused on Pyongyang?"

"Let's give it a go," Leticia said, assigning that task to individuals in the room. Damian went back to work as the Special Agent conferred with her Director. They were running out of time. They would soon have to notify the President and Congress of a potential problem, or they would be derelict in their duties. They also didn't want to look foolish by saying something was going to happen that wasn't. This particular something, if leaked to the public, would cause widespread panic and racial targeting of Asian people that might not even be Korean.

In a conference with other agencies in the room, they gave themselves an end time of five that evening to decide if to report.

Damian was trying to decide how to get the information for the country yet not reveal his source – a vast private facial recognition database that he had no plans to share with the rest of the world. He looked up the date of the last attempted hack. Then he pulled up satellite images from around the factory for a week before and after. He wouldn't tell people in the room how he had access to government spy satellites. He then ran all the images through his facial recognition software to see what came up. The vast majority of those identified seem to be workers. One name caused concern.

He looked up and realized he again had blocked out the room as he searched for information. People were leaning together over computers, and small group conversations were taking place. About two hours had passed since he made the suggestion. He needed to stand up and stretch. Get a little exercise.

"Does General Thae Yong-hol present any concerns? He was seen going into the factory around the time Viramic was hacked."

Damian winced as he watched a few heads turn so fast, that he feared whiplash. There was a little grumbling, and then Agent Ortiz spoke over the murmurs.

"That's a question for our North Korean expert. Mr. Kim, any thoughts about the General?"

Damian liked that Agent Ortiz didn't waste his time by making him explain where he got that information. That was the sign of a secure leader, or maybe she just had confidence in his knowledge.

"A brief bit of information about North Korea. It's a military state. It makes military vehicles and weapons and sells them to terrorist groups around the world. It has a lot of Generals and Admirals – our most recent estimates are of about twelve-hundred leaders. Being a General has perks, and you may eventually serve the supreme commander, but that happens only when you're much older – many of the Generals that serve Kim Jong-un are in their sixties. Generals that show anything but love and devotion for Kim disappear. Sometimes they die, are killed, or we suspect they are reassigned to remote labor camps. Generals have been known to try and get the attention of Kim by doing a 'good deed' for the country. So, this may be a case of some crazy general trying to impress Kim or otherwise stand-out. Mr. Green, can you find a connection between the General and a biology lab in North Korea?"

"Do you have a location for such a lab? Geo-coordinates would be great."

"We know of at least five labs. We also have tested the blood of North Korean defectors and found Smallpox antibodies in them, even though Smallpox is considered eradicated at the moment. So that suggests that they have a sample of it."

"Okay, give me the locations of the five labs, and I'll look for the General. Is there any chance someone would work on it outside of one of these labs?" Damian asked.

"I think anything possible with North Korea, but secret work outside of the labs is highly unlikely. The supreme leader is supreme, which means no one should outdistance him on intelligence or anything else," Kim said.

Damian nodded and went to work. He felt someone standing behind him and said, "Look, if you want official information, use your staff. If you want answers, let me do my thing. You may not watch how I search. Am I clear?" Damian said, getting ready to pack up and leave.

"Yes, yes, please sit down, Mr. Green. We'll clear everyone around you. I don't care where you get information on the North Koreans as long as you get it," said the FBI Director. This guy that Special Agent Ortiz had found was one of the most brilliant computer scientists that he had seen in a long time or perhaps ever. She provided him with a biography on Damian Green. They knew the man couldn't be bought with promises of money or prestige. It was best to get some work out of him while they could and tap him in the future when they had a critical need.

Damian worked for another two hours in silence on his part and found the information they were looking for.

He looked up and listened for a moment at the conversation taking place in the room. He'd been so focused on finding particular information about the Biolabs, that they could have been talking about a nuclear strike for all he paid attention.

The Special Agent must have been keeping an eye on him as she called out, "Mr. Green, have you found something?"

"Please call me Damian. Mr. Green is beginning to sound tedious. Yes, I've found the General visiting one of the biological labs. Agent Ortiz, I've sent the picture to you if you want to put it on the big screen. I don't know that I can do anything more for you on this case, as I can't read any of their communications."

Again, he began packing up to leave the group only to be halted by the Agent.

"Please stay, I may have something in mind. Let's just take a moment and talk about the implications of the photo. Clearly, the General is visiting a biological lab but isn't everything run by the military. Might this be the normal course of business?"

"It might be," said Lee. "But the lab is under a specific organizational structure, and it would be unusual for the General to visit such a lab that was not under his control. My latest speculative North Korea Leadership chart shows the General commanding a branch of the army. He has nothing to do with the lab. Of course, he might have other military reasons to visit. Has he repeatedly visited or just once?"

"Just once, for the time frame I looked at which was a week before and after his visit to the factory, which he also seems to have no reason to visit. Give me a moment, and I'll do a search to answer your question."

Damian tuned out the room again as he went in search of an

answer to the question of the General. He was vaguely aware of a debate as to whether this was enough information to go on high alert for the United States. The situation was labeled a 'severe threat' by Homeland Security.

Twenty minutes later, he had his answer.

"The General has made several visits to the lab."

"Can you tell us where the recent arrivals from North Korea have gone? You mentioned you looked at Canada and Mexico in addition to the United States."

"I would defer to your agencies. Wouldn't multiple government agencies know where these people have gone? Don't you randomly track the few North Korean visitors that arrive in North America?"

Damian thought he could get the information, and he knew he should do it on behalf of national security. Still, he didn't want to show his cards as to how powerful his computing system was.

"You're correct that there are several agencies that are probably tracking that information. However, it appears more and more like there's an imminent strike coming at us. I think you could get me the information a whole lot faster and probably more updated. These visitors are surely moving around, and the last thing we need is a static picture that's out of date."

Damian nodded, knowing she was right, and he went to work, getting his computer to track the requested information. Then, he decided to check with Ariana on how everyone was doing on the island. He tried to make the call but found his phone blocked. His computer was locked down while it was searching, so nobody could get into it while he was out of the room. He took his phone and stood up to go outside. Ortiz followed him out the door.

"Phones are blocked as this is a highly confidential conversation in the room. I'm just making sure you understand that not a word of what is going on inside is spoken to anyone else."

"If you asked me to leave the case, you wouldn't have to worry about me and confidentiality."

"Ah, but our national security is at risk, and you appear to be the Ferrari of finding information. I'm surrounded by a sea of four-door sedans that will get me there, but the race will be long over when that happens."

Damian smiled at her car analogy. He rather liked being called a Ferrari.

"I can help you as much by phone from my home as I can in person."

"It's good for the young guns to watch you. They were so full of themselves, and now they been put in their place. I don't suppose you would run an academy for intelligence officers on how to find information on the web?"

"No, not that it's any business of yours, but I'm calling Ariana to see how my business is going. I suspect she knows as much about this case as I do."

"Tell her I said hi!" the agent said as she turned and walked back inside the conference room.

He walked down to the cafeteria, testing to see if his phone had reception. He was relieved to know that it did. He would have hated going outside and then get stuck and be unable to get back through security again. Just before he made the call, his phone buzzed that someone was trying to get into his computer. He was happy to see them repelled. He continued to an unoccupied part of the cafeteria and called Ariana.

"Hey, what's going on?"

"It's looking more and more like the North Koreans may be gearing up for a biological strike. How is it there? Quiet, I hope?"

"Yes. No random visitors to the island. Your crew is working hard. Hermione and Jacob have a prototype of the app ready for testing. It isn't pretty yet, but they're testing to see if it works as planned. Tomorrow, I assume you'll be back, and Lily and I will go with the two teenagers to a few stores and test things out and protect them."

"I don't like that, but I don't know what to do differently. I'd give you pepper spray guns to take with you, but I don't want to get Lily in trouble since she's an ex-convict. Just promise me you'll leave if you see anybody in silver and blue clothing."

"Will do. Will you be back tonight, or should I take Hermione home with me?"

"Take her home with you since you're coming back in the morning. She knows where the spare watercraft garage remote is to close up the dock."

Damian's dock folded up into the lower level of his house so that it looked like there was no way onto the island other than landing on the beach and scrambling over the rocks to reach the top of the island.

Damian got a notice that his computer was done and so he ended the call with, "See you tomorrow, got to run."

He returned to the conference room and approached his computer. He looked around, planning on glaring at anyone that looked guilty perhaps because they might have tried to access his computer in his absence. Everyone had their head down working, though Ortiz saw him re-enter the room.

He had his computer convert the list of locations the North Korean visitors were to a map. Then he sent the map to the guy connected to the projector, and soon the entire room was looking at the map.

Damian said, "It appears they have plans for Canada as well as the United States, if indeed they are infected, or are carrying an infectious agent."

"There is one here in San Francisco, let's grab her and find out what she's up to," said the FBI Director.

"Be aware that she has an Indonesian Passport, but my facial recognition system identifies her as North Korean. You'll want to check on that before you get too far down the road interrogating her," Damian advised.

CHAPTER 24

Damian managed to wrangle out of the clutches of Special Agent Ortiz after turning over the data to her people to run down.

"I can't see a reason that I'll be back here again. If you need anything, you can reach me by phone, text, or email. Good luck," were his words as he left.

It has been a long day, and while he was delighted he could contribute to the national security of the United States, Damian questioned why these agencies weren't training their own people and developing their own systems as he had done.

Oh well, it wasn't his problem to solve, he was on to worrying about Hermione and Jacob. He also knew he needed to do another run for Natalie. He was proud when Agent Ortiz mentioned that the detective had found something his computer hadn't – the killer was stalking cat costumed people on the floats, Natalie had boots on the ground smarts. She studied information and complimented his ability to process data. Ortiz would have been smart to hire her to work on the Viramic case.

He looked at his watch and wondered where Ariana and Hermione were? Perhaps they were out on the Bay as he was, or maybe they were already home. He checked the GPS on Hermione's phone and saw indeed they were already home in Belvedere. Damian moved his boat to a higher speed aiming for his island. Even though he left it just that morning, it felt like a homecoming to see the beacon atop his island in the distance. A short time later, he was pulling the boat into the watercraft garage and pulling in his dock again for the night. He texted Ariana and Hermione that he was home, and he would see them in the morning. He went upstairs to his kitchen, uncorked a beer, and went outside to sit and watch the remainder of the sunset from his reclining chair, as the cats arrived for attention.

He contemplated his life nine years ago when he would have arrived home to Jen and the girls. Even three years ago, when he rarely left his island, the Richmond harbormaster was the most frequent visitor. His life was filled with people now. He thought he likely had an extraordinary talent for computers. He wasn't sure he would have discovered that in his old life if he hadn't spent months and years alone tinkering with data.

He sat straighter in his chair, jostling one of the cats off of his lap. He did a virtual slap across his face thinking about his day. All that he had come to care about – Ariana, Hermione, his employees, Natalie, Pete, and even the harbormaster were at risk by this potential North Korean threat. He needed to think about this case and work on it all night. He'd been lackadaisical in his approach, as it seemed far off. Damian knew Viramic had a solution, but that didn't mean that everyone that he cared about would get the treatment in time. That needed to be his top priority at the moment. Natalie's serial killer wouldn't affect him as no one was going to be on a float anytime soon. The BlueSilver CEO might be a threat, but it was second compared to an unleashed virus.

Damian stood up and went inside with the cats, feeding them and himself before heading down to his lab for a long night's work. He started by working on a dossier for each of the North Korean visitors. Then he moved on to the labs, thinking about what he should know about them. He studied the North Korean health care system, wondering what needs the country had for biology labs. They were able to test for hepatitis, tuberculosis, and HIV. Testing positive for HIV was the fastest way to get expelled from the country. Forty-Five percent of men were terrible smokers, so they had a lot of health care issues that followed the high smoking rate.

Damian moved on to read different articles discussing North Korea's biological weapons efforts. There was speculation that the country was experimenting with such weapons. There was concern that they had a small sample of Smallpox as defectors showed smallpox antigens in their blood, but really couldn't they have gotten that from a vaccine? He couldn't think of anything else to research, so he moved the information on to Special Agent Ortiz. It was two in the morning, perhaps he would get some sleep.

He was on his way upstairs when his cell phone rang, and the caller id said it was Agent Ortiz.

"You couldn't stay away from this investigation, huh?"

"More like I realized it might have an impact on people I care about, so I did more research, but nothing helpful to confirm or deny the presence of an infectious agent."

"Thanks to your earlier information we picked up the recent arrival to the San Francisco area. She claims to be a Chinese citizen though both you and our intelligence apparatus identify her as North Korean. We found nothing on her person or in her hotel room that has bothered us. We took blood from her to see if she's infectious, and we're doing a C.T. scan looking for any implants. I should know something within the hour."

"Could North Korea place agents here, then ship something to them?"

"Probably, anything is possible. It seems like you could ship to a port in a shipping container, some kind of bacteria as long as it was hardy enough to survive weather conditions. I'm not sure how we would find such a shipment. North Korea has a few allies in the world – China, Libya, South Africa. They could probably route a shipment through those countries and then on to the United States."

"There have to be some means of communication with these operatives for whatever North Korea plans. That's is what we need to find. This woman says she is just a Chinese citizen, right? What's her reason for visiting the United States? What do your Chinese interpreters think of her Chinese accent? Is it legitimate, or does Chinese sound like the second language she learned?"

"They don't think she's native to China as she can speak, but not read, Chinese, which is unusual given the breath of her vocabulary."

"Is there anything more I can do for you?" Damian asked.

"Do you think you could intercept communication going to any of these operatives?"

"I don't know. I'll try to do that."

"Call me if you find anything."

"Of course."

The call ended, and Damian glanced at the clock, debating what to do. Should he try for three to four hours sleep, or start his search for communication between these operatives and the mother country? He wasn't tired yet, and he was curious to see what he could do. It was like a test of his computer abilities, and it might be for one of the most complex searches ever.

Again he was hampered by the lack of language skills for these two languages, so he started with the passport cards they filled out when they arrived at the three countries' airport. The country code for North Korea was 850, and the area code was two. So then he looked for calls into the cities where these passengers arrived. Maybe he would get lucky and be able to hack into their communications.

Damian did a quick check of the time and saw it was already approaching six in the morning. He felt like he'd been sitting forever, and he decided he needed a swim. He put on his wet-suit and grabbed his snorkel and facemask. It was about a one-mile swim and would take him between thirty and forty minutes, depending on the waves.

An hour later, he was showered, shaved, fed, and had a large cup of coffee as he put his dock out to welcome his employees for the day as well as Ariana and Hermione. He went back to work until he heard his motion detectors indicate the approach of a boat. He went outside to assist Ariana in docking and tying her boat. He leaned down to kiss her and give Hermione a hug.

As Hermione made her way inside, Ariana paused and commented, "Your eyes are bloodshot. Did you stay up working all night?"

"Yes, my conscience was weighing on me. I have to save all of you from whatever North Korea has planned. I've been trying to hack into North Korean communications, and then I also did a swim around the island."

"So, you probably want all of us out of your hair today."

"I do, but you can't always get what you want, as Mick Jagger says. It's okay. I'll multitask. Maybe I'll ask Jordan to help me as he's the most computer savvy. It's just that I can't explain why I'm looking into North Koreans as we can't let the word out about what they may be doing in case it's wrong."

"You're between a rock and a hard place. You need help, and you probably need sleep, but you can't explain why you need those things until you figure out what's going on," Ariana said.

"Yep," he smiled tiredly and followed her inside to the lab where Hermione was already at work. He asked Hermione, "What are you testing today?"

"Jacob and I made an ugly and clunky copy of the future application, and we want to test it in the store to see if it blocks the signals and allows coupons through as promised. This is all about where the coding we've done is correct. We're going to different locations of the same stores to see if that works."

Damian nodded and said to Ariana, "You're the teens' driver, and Lily is their chaperone?"

"Yes, but I'm going inside as well. When the teens go down an aisle, Lily and I will each have a shopping cart, and we'll try to block anyone getting close to Hermione and Jacob."

"Sounds like a plan," Damian said. He heard his alarm go off and glanced to verify that it was the harbormaster delivering his employees.

Shortly the lab was crowded with the nine people at work that day. He left the door open to the dock, and that brought in enough cool air to offset the body heat. After grabbing more coffee, everyone settled into their routine and got to work. Damian returned to trying to decipher Korean messages. He then wrote a program that would go out and grab all calls between North America and North Korea. He translated them and passed them on to Special Agent Ortiz. She at least had something to act on.

CHAPTER 25

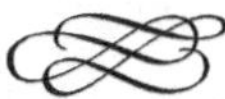

Fred Rodgers read the latest report from his two detectives and then smashed his fist on the table. It seemed like the company had disappeared overnight. No one was coming and going to the building, and no one at the attached restaurant knew where the company went. Fred knew he could torch the warehouse, but that wouldn't take down the makers of the app. His life's work was threatened by a teenager, who was likely going to earn ninety-nine cents every time he lost one of his million-dollar retail customers. It was so unfair.

He was going to have to hire a different group of people to track down the company and their employee home addresses. He was sure they could squeeze the information out of the staff. Meanwhile, he did a search for Damian Green's address. It would save him investigator dollars if he could find the address himself.

An hour later, he had nothing. Either the guy was renting or hiding behind a corporate name. It just made him all the angrier that he couldn't find anything personal on the guy. He found patents and a few other business milestones, but nothing beyond that. He considered himself to be a computer expert as he created this company. Sure it had been his college roommate's idea and coding, but that guy had no vision, and he hadn't made the company into what it was today.

Fred continued to search in frustration for information about Damian Green. It was like he was a made-up person. If he hadn't had patents in his name, he would've thought it was a fake name. After another hour of fruitless searching, he gave up. It was time to find help in the dark web, a place he occasionally visited when he was looking for something that wasn't entirely legal. If he was willing to pay in Bitcoin, he could find anything he needed in this obscure corner of the Internet.

He searched for investigators, except this time it was investigators willing to break the rules. If someone needed to be threatened in order to gain information, then this type of investigator would go there.

Then Fred sat back to think whether he wanted to threaten information out of people or just blow up the entire facility when everyone was inside it? Depending on how fast the work was going on the app, wasting time getting information on the company might not make sense. Yeah, the more he thought about it, the more he wanted to drop a nuclear bomb on the facility. He spent time studying the warehouse and surrounding area as he bet that Damian and his staff would eventually return. He would leave the old investigator group on the job to notify him when they re-inhabited the building.

Meanwhile, he asked for a very different type of service from the dark web. He decided he wanted a bomb expert that could blow up the building and its occupants once they returned. Consolidated Security gave him a rough floor plan of the warehouse, and he determined that if the bomb expert couldn't get inside, that there were other options.

Fred made the arrangement to pay in Bitcoin, and he was done for the day. Maybe this entire ugly scenario would be over soon. Indeed, he would have to cut back on his toys as the bomb expert took all of his spare cash for this task.

CHAPTER 26

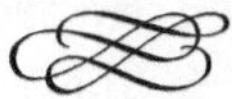

General Thae Yong-ho oversaw a secret dispersion of people to North America. They traveled under a variety of passports that he'd had made in one of the Pyongyang factories. He was the leader of one of North Korea's feared labor camps. Prisoners were worked up to sixteen hours a day while being starved at the same time. He hated managing the boring camps, and he became immune to the suffering and death after several years. He saw other generals be promoted to better assignments. He had begun to plan what he could do to stand out among the generals and finally get that promotion that was his due. He studied the regime and determined that his Marshal wanted leverage over the West, which he considered the enemy. So the General had quietly plotted to get his Marshal that leverage.

A cargo ship was coming into port in a city called Houston that was in the center of the United States. In the cargo hold was a series of cans that said cleaning spray on the outside, but on the inside contained a new virus that scientists said was very infectious. He planned to have someone in the port of Houston unpack the boxes and mail to his people around North America. They were to then take the bottles while wearing face masks and spray them in crowded indoor places while cleaning high surfaces. That way, the droplets would stay in the air. His people would look like they were cleaning, while in actuality, they will be spraying the deadly virus around. He pulled people from his labor camps who had a family he could threaten. He had the added benefit of these operatives getting away from the camp. Should they say the wrong thing or run away, any remaining family would be terminated.

It was a plan that had been seven years in the making. The General was so close to hitting the button that would destroy the West, that he could barely contain his grins outside his residence. It was time to tell his Marshal. Again he'd schemed how to get close to the Marshal to tell him about the plan. He didn't want more powerful and popular generals to take credit for his hard work. Today was a government meeting where they all spoke about their accomplishments, so he was going to announce it there in public. He hoped it would be a bombshell. He didn't see any other way to deliver his news and still get credit by the Marshal. Of course, there was a risk that the Marshal would hate his plan, but he didn't see that happening. The Marshal was famous for his hate of the West. This time he didn't have to fire missiles to threaten people; instead, he could just unleash a virus on them, cause death, and destroy their economy. What wasn't to like about the plan?

The General practiced his speech in his mirror at home before coming to the meeting. He was ready and awaiting his turn to give his report on the camp. He was quick to recite the numbers of work hours that had been achieved by the prisoners as well as the number of deaths, and then he added his unexpected news, quickly and thoroughly laying out his plan. The Marshal had a variety of emotions flit across his face. It took him some time to figure out how he felt.

"You say you have operatives ready to spread an as yet unknown infection to the three countries of North America?"

"Yes, Sir.

"Why did I not know about your actions before now?"

Now came the tricky part... how to compliment the supreme ruler while showing his own brilliance to everyone.

"Marshal, I didn't want to bother you until I had sufficient resources in place to make sure this operation would happen. The last major step was our operatives arriving in North America and getting through immigration. That has happened, and we will be able to spread the viral agent in about three days for the United States and a little longer for Canada and Mexico. Do you wish to proceed?"

"No," came the fast response that surprised the General.

"What...Why?"

"If we disperse a deadly agent in the United States and they notice all of a sudden that lots of people are dying in their major cities and they discover the source, they will drop a nuclear bomb on North Korea and erase this country off the face of the earth. Mr. Yong-ho, call back your operatives."

Oh no, the General thought, this wasn't going as planned. The fact that the Marshal used the term 'Mr.' meant that he was about to lose the title of 'General', and he was going to end up probably in his own detention camp. He was so embarrassed to lose face in front of so many of his colleagues. He reddened and stood up bowing to the Marshal.

"I shall do as you ask," he said, coming out of the bow and making to leave the room.

He stepped outside and saw nothing but a very bleak future. He'd entered the room giddy with what he had done, and now he plunged to the bottom. Before giving it much thought, he pulled the small pistol at his side, aimed at his head and fired.

The conference room door opened, and several officers rushed out with weapons pulled, ready to protect their Marshal. Instead, they found General Yong-hol lying in a pool of blood. An officer bent down to feel for a pulse and said, "He's still alive."

"Shoot him again, let's make sure he's dead," the Marshal said.

"But Marshal, I don't think he had time to call off his operation."

"True, still shoot him again. I'll call the United States and warn them of what may be happening. I'll call him a rogue officer, and plead with them not to hit their nuclear button. If he were to recover from the gunshot, he wouldn't do so in the next three days by the look of it, so I don't think he'll be of help to us."

The Marshal continued back to his office, worried about what might be unleashed on his enemies that would come back to haunt him. He called out orders to track the General's communications and find out who the operatives were that left North Korea.

He settled in his office with a translator and called the President of the United States. This was not a call he was looking forward to.

He was shocked to find that the American President had already been warned by his intelligence agency of a possible strike. They had also reached out to Canada and were trying to determine if Mexico was in danger. The Marshal was embarrassed to learn more about his rogue General's plan from the Americans, then he learned from the General himself.

The United States requested the Marshal release a group of ten people, all relatives of one of the General's operatives currently in American custody. Once South Korea confirmed the arrival of the family members by video call, the agent would talk.

The Marshal would have kicked the dead General's body if he had access to it. He hated doing the work requested by the Americans, but he needed to grovel if he didn't want his country blown to bits.

The Marshal had one more call with the Americans, and then

he was able to hand the problem off to a staff member. The Americans thought they knew where all the operatives were, but they didn't know where the infectious agent was.

CHAPTER 27

Natalie had been back from Copenhagen for a few days. She thought that Damian might have time to make another projection of where next their serial killer would strike. She had added depth to the details of more cases, and of course, there was the added discovery of the target being a cat costumed float character. She added columns to the spreadsheet he'd initially given her, so he would haven't to enter that new information into his computer, before rerunning the same prediction program. She picked up her phone and called him.

Once he answered, she asked, "Have you saved the United States from North Korea?"

"I can neither confirm nor deny that the United States is at risk from North Korea."

"You had fun saying that line, didn't you?"

"It was rather fun," Damian said, and Natalie could hear the smile in his voice. That was a good thing.

"Did you see the modified spreadsheet I sent you? Can you enter that information into your big computer in the sky, and give me an answer as to where he'll strike next?"

"Actually, you caught me at a good moment. I'll stop what I'm doing and work on your stuff. I'll call you back in an hour with your answer."

"Thanks, Damian. Good to know that I'm not likely going to die before I close this cold case."

"No, I suspect you have a long retirement in front of you, Natalie."

The line went dead, and Natalie had to smile. She knew enough about the issue with North Korea to be worried, but not enough to throw her into a full-scale panic.

She thought about what else she might contribute to the case. Did their killer have a routine with the murder weapon? Inevitably, after all of these years, he'd run out of new ways to kill and had begun to recycle older methods. She looked at the two most recent years of deaths, but there was no pattern to the murder weapon. He would do the same thing twice in a row and then not use a method for a year. She put it aside and decided to wait on the call from Damian.

It turned out that she didn't have long to wait. First, her email dinged, and then her cell phone lit up with Damian's number.

"My computer is picking the Tel Aviv Roaring Railroad parade. There's a float entry from last year that is all cats. It's a parade that celebrates the start of summer for children, so many characters are on floats."

"Wow, that's taking a big chance. Israel is known for its police always being on the lookout for terrorists. I don't recall if there's been another suspected float death in Israel."

"There was a prior death in Jerusalem according to the printout. I wonder if it took him that long to find a parade there, or if he randomly pulls a city out of a hat then has to find a parade there with a cat character, or as you say maybe he went after more low hanging fruit in cities without superior detective divisions."

"Okay, well, I guess I'll call Special Agent Ortiz. It will be interesting to work with the Israelis. I wonder if I'll get to go there.

Hopefully, with their superior detection, this will become the killer's last murder."

"I would hope. Good luck, Natalie."

"Thanks for all you do, Damian."

Natalie called her Lieutenant just to let him know of the next suspected murder location.

"Tel Aviv? That takes some guts. That's like trying to pit yourself against the best for additional thrills."

"Yes, isn't it? Will the department fund travel to Israel if I get invited by Special Agent Ortiz?"

"Yes. Your findings could lead to the capture of this killer, and even if they want to try him in Israel, I would think the United States could extradite him here as we have several homicides, whereas hopefully, Israel only has an attempted murder. We haven't verified if the prior death in Jerusalem was the killer's work."

"Good point, Lieu. Okay, I'll keep you posted."

Next, Natalie called Special Agent Ortiz.

"Agent Ortiz, are you available to talk at the moment, or are you tied up with the other problem?"

"Both. What's up, Natalie?"

"Damian did a run for me, and our next target is a children's parade in Tel Aviv, Israel."

"Wow," the Agent said with a wealth of meaning, impressed with the killer's latest target. "When is the date of that parade?"

"We have about nine days as it's the last Saturday in June. What would you like to do?"

Ortiz thought about what she was juggling with the North Korean case. She thought she would be done with the locating the infectious agent, or the world would change drastically and the serial killer wouldn't matter in the greater scheme of things.

"Give me two days, then I'll go through channels and set up a meeting with the Israelis. Would you like to join me?"

"Yes, please. The department will fund my travel to Israel in the hopes that we capture this guy. My Lieutenant said that in theory, the killer would be up for attempted murder charges there, whereas, in the United States, he will have multiple murder charges. Of course, if we validate that the death in Jerusalem was his work, then the Israelis can charge him for murder."

"Yes, hopefully, they will agree with us. They could also charge the killer with terrorism, which would get him a sentence of at least forty years. I'd be happy with that. Let Israel pay for the cost of housing him in prison. The United States would want time with him to see if we could get him to confess to his crimes. It would be nice to solve all of those cold cases for both the families and the police forces."

"True. As long as he was locked away. We would have validation of what crimes he committed in the U.S. I would be good with that as would the Justice Department, I think."

"Okay, I'll give you a call as soon as I find a shipment today or tomorrow, and we'll plan our approach to the Israelis."

"Thanks, Special Agent."

"It's Leticia, Natalie, and I'll talk to you soon."

Natalie ended the call with the thought of preparing to travel to Israel in a few days. They might be there for a few days as they planned the killer's capture or even maybe spy him upon one of the country's famous Hawk-Eye surveillance cameras that are ever-present and looking for terrorists. Now was the moment she should go spend some time with her husband before she got the call from the Special Agent to race across the world again, she thought with a smile of anticipation.

CHAPTER 28

Leticia was deep into leading her team at the FBI's San Francisco Office when her Director was called to the phone for a classified briefing. She knew it was highly likely that the phone call from Washington, DC had an impact on her current case. While her Director was gone, she received a call from Damian Green, who had some new data.

"Hello, Special Agent. I have some information I intercepted between North Korea and these operatives that suggests that whatever is about to go down will do so in about three days after a ship docks in Houston. I don't have the name of the ship or its exact arrival time, but perhaps that is less of a needle in a haystack to look for this infectious agent. To aid you, I have a list of planned ship arrivals at the Port Of Houston during the next thirty-six hours. Perhaps you can do something with that?"

"Yes, that's is very helpful. I'll get my crew working on the ships. Of course, some of these ships have eight to ten-thousand shipping containers, but maybe we can get dogs to smell them or X-ray them. Are any of the arriving ships coming in from China?"

"Yes, but keep in mind that North Korea has other friends besides China."

"Okay, thanks. Keep working and send me any other information you have."

Leticia ended the call as she was watching the Director approach her with some new news clearly on his face. He motioned her over so they could have a private conversation away from everyone working in the conference room.

"I just got a call from Washington. The President received a call from Kim Jong-un about an infectious agent that one of his Generals planned to release in the U.S. They are running it down on their end, but the General committed suicide, so they are missing some key information. Basically, we had Kim in the position of begging us not to drop a nuclear bomb on his country. Those in on the call demanded the release of the family members related to our prisoner. We are supposed to have them moved to South Korea within the hour. Then, we'll video conference our suspect with her family and see if she'll then spill her guts as to where the infectious agent is."

"My computer expert deciphered some of the North Korean communications, and he says those communications point to a ship arriving into the Port of Houston within the next thirty-six hours that contains the virus. He also ran a list of ships arriving at the port, figuring it's in one of those large container ships. The trouble is those ships hold up to ten-thousand containers, so we will have to quarantine ships and find a way to search for the agent."

"At least we're getting closer. Perhaps without the General giving directions, nothing will happen. The product will sit in an obscure container without anyone retrieving it. Did you request the SIC in Houston roust the troops to be intercepting these ships?"

"I was about to do that when you called me over, Sir. We also need to apprehend all of the other operatives, so someone needs to contact Mexico and Canada. I'll contact my counterparts in those countries, while you alert our offices across the United States to secure these operatives."

They both spent the next hour on the phone in their assigned tasks. Meanwhile, the U.S. Embassy in Seoul was ready to connect the family to the person presently in their building in custody. The agent and the Director facilitated that conversation. Unfortunately, all they learned was she was expected to get a package in the next three to four days, but she didn't know where it was coming from or who mailed it.

This General had planned his scheme well as it was hard to stop it once it went into motion. Thankfully, North Korea didn't happen to want war at this moment in time and was doing everything possible to find the toxic agents.

Leticia thought of something else and decided Damian might be faster at giving her an answer than her own people, so she called him.

"Yes?"

"Did the General visit any factories or shipping places? I'm wondering if we can find a few companies to focus on among all the ships going into the Port of Houston."

"Are you sure about the Port of Houston? Maybe my data is wrong," Damian said.

"We got the North Korean operative to talk. She explained that she was supposed to stay at her location for three to four days, and then she would receive a package with instructions. She didn't know what was in the package to the point that she didn't know that there was an infection in the package, let alone, how she was going to share it. Your clue about Houston is the best clue we have."

"Okay. I'll see what I can do and call you back."

"Thanks."

Leticia knew the Director would be leaving for Houston, if for no other reason than to be in on the photo opportunity of standing close to an infectious agent that his staff found. She wasn't being cynical, she would have done the same thing. She updated him on the new information she hoped to have by the time he reached Houston.

Leticia had her people working on ship bills of lading, which should have the shipper names. Leticia pulled in the Coast Guard to make ship calls asking for the documentation before they reach the port. It would be the Director's call if the United States was to demand that the ships remain outside of Galveston in the Gulf of Mexico. Further complicating finding the infectious cargo was that there were two ports in the Houston area – Barbours Cut and Bayport. They didn't know which port the ship was set to dock at. Direct shipping from North Korea was illegal, so the shipment would have to go through another country. It might be China or South Korea or some other country. She really hoped that Damian might come up with a company name. Otherwise, they were back to looking for a needle in a haystack given multiple container ships and the fact they were probably looking for a reasonably small package.

Her phone lit up, and she punched the green button.

"Yes."

"I don't know why I didn't think of this before, but I think you should focus on a company named Naegohyang. That's the company that tried to hack into Viramic, and it makes a variety of products. If you have established contact with the North Korean government, they should be willing to contact that company and see if they know where the package is."

"That's brilliant, and you're right. I don't know why I didn't think of doing that. My only excuse is I haven't had much sleep in the last few days. I'll get on that. Is your computer still checking satellite pictures?"

"It is, but it will be tedious as in theory, a General would have personal errands to run like going to a grocery store, so separating the personal from this plot is not simple."

"Yes, you're correct. Let's hope we have the right company, and we can go from there."

She ended her call and then contacted the Director, who was still in the air to Houston.

"Do you have something for me?"

"Possibly," Leticia said, explaining Damian's theory and the problem with using satellite images. "Can we ask North Korea to contact the company and get the answer for us?"

"Sounds simple enough. I'll get on that, and we'll find out just how cooperative Kim Jong-un is."

They ended the call, and Leticia had her people focus on bill of lading for the company Damian named.

She struck gold when they found a shipment in a container of a ship at Bayport that was in the process of being unloaded.

From there, things quickly came together. The Director received confirmation from North Korea that they had the right shipment. The North Korean company CEO gave a description of what the package looked like. Multiple federal agencies swarmed the port setting up a hazardous materials container zone as the box was located, and hermetically sealed. It was then transported to the Level 4 biological lab in Galveston so scientists could figure out what was in the package. Other officials from the CDC started a painstaking process of determining if the entire shipping container was contaminated and possibly the whole cargo ship.

Leticia was simply happy that the infection hadn't reached the citizens she served. It was time to move her focus back to the serial killer and make contact the Israelis.

CHAPTER 29

Lily and Ariana had trailed the two teens as they tested their initial crude phone application through many aisles of four stores. They bought a few items at each store as payback for being able to test their technology though the stores did not notice what the two teens were up to, other than they were watching the phones even more than the usual phone obsession that teens had.

They got what they needed. Ariana dropped off Jacob and Lily at their home before heading for the Richmond Marina and back to Red Rock Island. They arrived just as the others were leaving to return to the same marina. It was a comical boat traffic jam. It cleared, and then Ariana and Hermione went inside Damian's lab, where he was stretching, yawning, and smiling all at the same time.

"You look happy," Ariana said, leaning in for a quick kiss.

"We just saved millions of Americans, so as they say, it was a good day at the office."

"Millions, huh?" Hermione said, wondering what Damian was involved with now and thinking about the cold case. "That seems like a lot of parade float riders."

"Actually, it was a different case that you might hear about if you watched the news. I just helped the FBI find an infectious shipment sent to the United States by North Korea that was onboard a cargo ship in Houston."

"So Viramic is safe," Ariana said.

"Yes."

"How did you help them find the shipment?" Hermione asked. "Did you build a special infection detector?"

"No, but that's not a bad idea for a future project for this company. It could be used by customs to scan incoming products to the U.S.," Damian said, writing down the idea before continuing. "Actually, I had a Sherlock Holmes moment."

"Sherlock Holmes?" Ariana asked, puzzled.

Damian then explained the whole story about Viramic, and the wayward General and his suicide, and Kim Jong-un.

"So I thought of the company that tried to hack your start-up, and the bigwigs reached back through North Korea to confirm that that manufacturing company sent the package at the General's request. They found it on a cargo ship in the Houston harbor in the process of being unloaded. Many bigwigs and agencies rushed to Houston and contained the package, which is now with the CDC. Thus crisis averted, and we're all safe. My work is done for today," Damian said, still grinning with the memory of averting the crisis.

"So the Sherlock Holmes moment is what?" Hermione asked.

"It's elementary my dear Watson. I had the answer in front of me all along, I just needed to realized it."

"Good job! I'm glad we're all safe," Ariana said, patting him on the back.

"Yes, but is it safe to participate on a parade float?" Hermione asked.

"Depends on what costume you're wearing. Natalie discovered that all the victims were wearing some kind of cat costume as in lions, tigers, domestic cats, etc.. So as long as you're in a bear or dog costume, you'll be fine."

"Your killer sounds seriously creepy," Ariana said.

"I think you have to be a creepy sociopath to go on a twenty-year killing spree of something as harmless as parade float volunteers. Hopefully, my computer is correct in its prediction that the Tel Aviv Children's parade is next on his list, and the elite Israeli Police can stop him."

"How does your computer predict where he strikes next?" Hermione asked.

"I entered as much information about each case as I had, then wrote a program asking it to predict the next location. The last time it came me a forty percent chance of being right, and it was. It was the Copenhagen Carnival, and an officer rode the float in a cat queen costume and nearly died. He was handed a stick that was covered in fentanyl, and it quickly stopped his breathing. Fortunately, everyone was watching. He received emergency medical care, and he's fine. I think there must be a pattern to his targets that I can't see, but the computer uses it to predict the next location. It helped that Natalie was able to limit it to cat costumed characters on floats. That eliminates a fair number of parades."

"I wonder how your computer sees a pattern that you don't," Hermione pondered.

"I haven't had time to look for a pattern. Does the killer move from one continent to the next in a pattern? Is he going from big parades to small? Does he try and pick off a national hero/mascot? Whatever his pattern is, it's not obvious at a glance. Heck, I didn't even notice the cat costumed character trait about his victims. Natalie spent an entire day studying the data and came up with that one detail."

"So you're making progress with the help of computer and human intelligence. That's pretty cool," Hermione said.

"It's a reminder that neither computer nor human has all the answers, and they're best when they work together."

"So can you show me what you're doing to track the BlueSilver company? I'd like to learn to spy on everyone like you do, Damian," Hermione asked.

"You should only investigate people that you have a reason to think will harm you or friends that you're about to admit to your inner circle. Don't spy on people out of curiosity as it will wreck your life."

"That's good advice, Damian," Ariana agreed. "Right after Damian and I met for the first time, we both did searches on each other. We weren't looking for each other's secrets, I think we just wanted to know the other person wasn't a serial killer. Anything else about a friend will come out over time. It's a learning experience as you figure out how good your first impressions are of people. Make sense?"

"Yes. I won't pull out my yearbook and look up every person and their family, rather I'll wait for them to want to be more than a classmate."

"Exactly. Like I said, you'll be happier by not digging into every person's dirty laundry. So back to your question about BlueSilver. Here is what I've done to gather information."

Damian went on to describe how he was keeping tabs on Fred Rodgers.

"What don't you know about him?" asked Hermione.

"I don't know where he has gone on the dark web. If he has gone somewhere substantial, he could hire all sorts of horrible people."

"Why don't you know of what is going on in the dark web?" Hermione asked.

"Because that part of the web is not indexed, so it makes it hard to search."

"Is the dark web somewhat vast?

"There are estimates that put the normal web as a tiny portion of your entire internet, so it's hard to know how large it is."

"Is it all bad stuff?" Ariana asked. "I've never visited there to my knowledge, so I have no idea what it is like."

"You need a special encrypted browser like Tor. Tor stands for 'the onion router,' and the dark web uses onion or encrypted routing so that you can't be traced. There's a fair amount of criminal activity there, but also agencies like the CIA and FBI have websites inside the dark web so they can receive untraceable tips related to crime. Some large newspapers likewise have dark web locations so they can receive anonymous tips related to news stories."

"Okay," Hermione said after thinking about Damian's explanation. "So can you tell if someone has entered the dark web? Like Fred Rodgers?"

"You as a user can tell when you've crossed over and into the dark web, but I can't see you 'virtually knocking on the door' of the web. Does that make sense? Consider the dark web to be a black hole that you can't follow anyone through."

"So, for you to dig for information on BlueSilver, you mostly have to stay out of the dark web, right?"

"Right, it's too dark to see, so I can't follow anyone around. One thing I like to do whenever I'm investigating anyone is to check that person's finances. As money goes, so goes trouble. Following the money was how I found that the investigation company was hired. He used company money to do that, so it was easier to find. However, if we're looking at his private finances, that can be much harder to find. Also, services are bought with a cryptocurrency like Bitcoin on the dark web. So, if we see a Bitcoin purchase from his personal bank account that tells us exactly nothing about what he is purchasing."

"Wow, this is cool. I wish they taught this in school."

"No!" screeched both adults at once.

"Can you imagine how parents would react?" Ariana asked.

"Can you imagine the bullying that would go on if everyone

knew everyone else's business?" Damian said. "This may be interesting work, but remember what I said at the beginning. You don't do a search on everyone."

"Okay, you're right about the bullying. It's bad enough with all the technologies we have to screw ourselves up with."

"What I would like to know is how much he is discussing it within the company. I ghosted one of his employees and got his password to an email server. This is an illegal thing to do, and I'm not teaching you how to do it, so don't ask. I used the ghosting feature to tap into his email. Of course, I can only read what he has already read, as I don't want him to notice that his unread emails are becoming read. He's been getting reports from the private investigators that we disappeared, and no one knows where we went. The investigators are going through their pictures and trying to find the home addresses of our employees. That is not good, the game may be up soon, and I'll have to warn everyone about their security."

"I thought you added security to everyone's residence already," Ariana said.

"I told everyone that I would be happy to help them beef up their security, but no one felt in need of it as they hadn't suffered any break-ins or stolen packages."

"So have any of them suffered any thefts since then?" Ariana asked.

"Not that they have mentioned to me. Let me read further down to see if the investigators identified anyone."

There was silence in the lab as Damian continued reading.

"Okay, they identified all of us. The investigators are most distressed that while they identified me, they can't find where I live. Hooray for that! I'll move everyone back to the building as I think people are in no more danger at home than in our building. However, I'll make another offer on additional security."

"Are you concerned that they are still on the case?" Ariana asked.

"Yes and no. It feels personal now that that the investigators have identified everyone. At the same time, if I were in his position, I would have made the same investigative effort to see what we were up to. I just would have been more successful at it."

"So I think that's it for the night. Shall we make dinner?"

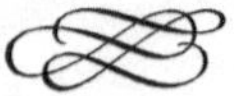

CHAPTER 30

Special Agent in Charge Leticia Ortiz used her connections within the FBI and State Department to make arrangements to meet with law enforcement in Tel Aviv, Israel. She could tell that the Israelis, like the Danish before them, were skeptical of such a weird story about a serial murderer. However, as they were flying into Tel Aviv and asking for a meeting with the police, Israel would honor the request.

Leticia and Natalie met at the San Francisco Airport, preparing for the long, fourteen-hour flight to a country that neither had visited before. Culturally, Leticia had tried to read about the customs before she arrived. Were they as women at a disadvantage? She didn't think so, as to the best of her knowledge, they wouldn't be entering a traditional orthodox neighborhood. The FBI representative assigned to the American Embassy would join them in the meeting, and he had been briefed on the issue. The American Ambassador to Israel was presently visiting the United States and was therefore unable to join them on short notice.

They were both able to get a little sleep on the long flight, and they arrived the next day in the late afternoon. By the time they got through customs, it was the dinner hour, and so they headed to their hotel to have a meal and go over the presentation for the next morning. The Tel Aviv FBI Attaché joined them for dinner to hear more about the case. His name was Agent Levy, and he had a good relationship with the Israeli Police.

"So as you probably know from your own research, the State of Israel has one police force that is divided up geographically. The Tel Aviv section is the second largest and the most densely populated. You'll be meeting at the Civic Center station, and the Tel Aviv Commander will be joining local leaders for this meeting."

"Do they have any belief in this case?" Natalie asked. "Or do they think we're American nutcases."

"They are too polite to call you a nutcase to your face, Detective. However, as Leticia suggested, I connected them to Constable Nielsen in Copenhagen, and that transformed their attitude. They are quite anxious to meet with you. My impression is they see an opportunity to globally shine by catching this guy who has eluded multiple countries."

"They may not feel that way when we point out to them that there was another parade murder here fifteen years ago in Jerusalem during a Purim parade. We haven't investigated the details of that case – to confirm whether the death was truly an accident or made to just look that way," Natalie said.

"Oh, I don't think they know this might not be the only case in this country. It's going to be an interesting morning."

"We don't speak Hebrew. I assume there won't be a problem having a conversation in English? I also assume that any police reports are written in Hebrew, so we would be unable to review their parade float death in Jerusalem," Agent Ortiz said.

"Yes, the police reports are in Hebrew, but you'll find most people proficient in reading Hebrew and translating it into English. English is considered a mandatory language for success in the business world, so you'll have no trouble following the conversation."

"How about street cameras and crime scene staff. In your opinion, are they good here?" Natalie asked.

"Yes. Some people feel that the cameras are too intrusive. Still, you should get excellent coverage of the parade route, which is right along the beach."

"Okay, I think we're good to go. Are you picking us up in the morning to take us to wherever the meeting is?"

"Yes. I'll be here at 7:30am. Don't be late. People are very punctual in this town, it's a cultural norm."

"Good to know. Thanks for stopping by, and we'll see you in the morning."

In minutes, the two women wrapped up their discussion and were in bed with alarms set for early the next morning. Both had requested wake up calls from the hotel in case their alarms failed them.

The next morning they hit rush hour traffic, which Natalie had read was some of the worse in the world. She had to say it was more gridlocked here in Tel Aviv than in Silicon Valley. They made it the short distance to the police building with Agent Levy leading the way. He had clearly been inside the building before and knew the process of getting upstairs. Around them, officers were going to and fro in a variety of sharp uniforms with side arms and other items on a utility belt. Natalie briefly wondered if it was shift change given the officer movement, or maybe she and Leticia were the source of curiosity.

They followed Agent Levy into a conference room where everyone stood at their arrival and were offered handshakes. Shortly, Leticia opened the meeting with research into their serial killer, and then Natalie's presentation. Natalie added a specific slide on the death in Jerusalem as an added potential concern for the Israeli Police. Her presentation was stopped at that point by questions and requests by the Commander.

"I have no recall of this death fifteen years ago, although it was in Jerusalem, which is an hour away. Can you give me more details?"

"I cannot, Sir. Given the large number of cases throughout the world, I focused on gaining more details from English speaking police department reports. It would have taken time to translate from Hebrew. If you could bring me the case file and serve as a translator, I believe I can quickly clarify if it was the work of our killer. You will see in my next slide that he has a particulate modus operandi. He selects victims that are fully costumed in some version of a cat. If your victim from Jerusalem was in a cat costume, then it's highly likely they were a prior murder."

With that explanation, the Commander directed one of his people to call the other police region and find those details.

"Please continue, Detective."

"I'm just about to wrap up with my final slide. We have a civilian computer expert that created a model to project the next murder. That model indicated it was the children's parade this weekend here in Tel Aviv, and so that is why we are here."

Leticia added, "Many countries have reason to try this criminal. As the United States has the most alleged murders by this killer, we would open negotiations with Israel to extradite him back to the United States. However, we have to catch him first, and we hope that our computer projection is correct. We would like to be a part of your planning. Through our work with the Danish Police, we learned our killer is a male, but more description than that we don't know."

"So you're saying that you have a computer model that predicts that someone riding on a float fully dressed in some kind of cat costume will be the target of your murderer?"

"Yes, Sir."

"Why don't we just ban all the cat costumed characters from the parade?"

"Certainly, that would keep Israel safe, but it won't help you with the death in Jerusalem if indeed that death is one of the victims," Leticia said.

The door to the conference opened and the person that the Commander had directed to research the death in Jerusalem, returned to his seat where he was met with expectant looks from those around the conference table.

"Status?" asked the Commander.

"Sir, the file is on its way here, but the victim on the float was wearing a cat costume."

"Okay, then let's put all of our resources into capturing this criminal. Tell me about the plan that the Danes used. We need to do better, and Chief Inspector Katz, find out how many floats have costumed cats on them."

"Sir, here is a list of methods by which his victims have died. We haven't determined a pattern, and so we won't guess what method he will use this time," Natalie said, handing over a piece of paper.

There was silence in the room as everyone waited while the Commander reviewed the list. Then he looked up and said, "What an evil person. He's killed children in the pursuit of his hatred of cat creatures. Hopefully, we catch him before anyone gets injured. I hope he uses one of the methods on this sheet that a police officer can be resuscitated back to the living. Maybe given that we have three or four days, we could have some engineers create protective suits for our people – like a lead-lined costume that is rubberized to prevent electrocution. I'll see what our lab can come up with once we know the extent of the costumes scheduled for floats."

"Has he killed anyone walking in a parade maybe along with a float or with a cast of characters?" Katz asked.

"No. Each of these deaths has resulted from being on a parade float. Know that our killer has already studied the float entries and likely has one picked out. Maybe Special Agent in Charge Ortiz could elaborate on the FBI's Behavioral Analysis Unit evaluation of our killer," Natalie said, thinking about what a mouthful of words had been her last sentence."

"How good are your city cameras around this city? Our killer is likely already here, though in disguise. If your cameras have built-in facial recognition software, we might find him before the start of the parade. We could take the pictures we had from the Copenhagen murder site and see if your software can find him in the city," Leticia suggested.

"On that," uttered Katz, as he stood up to leave the room again.

Over the next three days, the group in the conference room would plan what they were going to do on the day of the parade. Natalie received a full briefing about everything in the file from the Jerusalem float death. The Israeli Inspector agreed that the Jerusalem death was one of their serial killer's victims.

James King was enjoying his second visit to Israel. It had been fifteen years since he last visited the Israel. He just passed through this busy city at that time and he was surprised by the growth in buildings and traffic. He was impressed with the beauty of Tel Aviv with the Mediterranean Sea and the city's beaches. The restaurants were excellent and the people fascinating to watch on the promenades next to the beaches. Jerusalem, by contrast, was dry looking and mountainous. He'd taken the time when he visited the last time to go to the Dead Sea, which was dying as both the Israelis and Jordanians siphoned off the water from the Jordan River. The Dead Sea was not getting replenished at the rate it needed. He felt like he should stand on the hilltop above the Dead Sea and proclaim that he was the king of the Dead Sea as the killer of so many people. He stood there, smiling at the Sea for quite some time. He thought about revisiting it during this trip, but he really liked to explore countries when he was there for a parade. So this trip he was visiting Tel Aviv and Haifa. In fact, he arrived by boat from Cyprus to Herzliya, which was north of Tel Aviv, but south of Haifa. A perfect location from which to explore both cities and quietly enter Israel. He had four days to explore the county before the weekend parade, and if he played it right, he would be on board his yacht leaving the harbor before the parade ended. He didn't need to see the actual character die. He discovered that in a full costume, sometimes it was hard to tell if a character was dead or alive. Instead, he liked to find an article about the mysterious death and read the news the next day.

Avoiding the cameras in Israel was tricky as they were everywhere looking for terrorists. Of course, he was a terrorist of sorts. He'd killed a lot of people, just not at one time. When questioned by the Border guards at the port, he indicated that he was there to explore historic sites like Jaffa, Masada, the Mount of Olives, and the Western Wall. Reciting the names quickly and correctly convinced the border guard that he was serious about historic sites, and he was instantly approved for entry. For this trip, he used the passport belonging to Edward Roerden, one of ten passports that he rotated through for his kill travels. He stayed aboard his boat to keep his profile low and used sheruts to get around the country. Other than his entry into Israel, there was no record of Edward Roerden visiting places in the country.

Every day he took a walk along the promenade, where he planned to pick off the tiger on the next to the last float. He'd reviewed the order of the floats, which helped him decide which float to go after as more than one float had a cat character on it. However, in parades like this where he had a choice, he liked to choose floats later in the parade as some of the crowd dispersed by then. He wanted a crowd to hide in, but not a big group that might jostle him or observe him kill a float character. He also walked down each of the side streets from the parade route in case he had to make a quick escape. The police had never chased him, but he knew if he ever let his guard down and didn't thoroughly prepare, he would be caught. Overtime he perfected his routine with his pre-parade research. About a decade ago, when he had a scare at a parade, he had multiple disguises both before and during the parade. He had a series of layers made out of thin materials that he could remove as he walked. The seams were held together by Velcro, so he could walk and change clothing, hats, and hair.

Before he arrived in each country or city, he studied the efficacy of their police force. He wanted to keep killing as there were still parades that he hadn't visited. He wouldn't be finished until every cat costumed character was wiped off the face of the earth. James King hoped to kill them all before he died.

His mother had set him on this path over thirty years ago, and he wasn't done yet. His mother lit a spark in him that he had yet to extinguish. Simply wipe out every cat character that he wasn't invited to be, and since he started down the path at age twelve, no one had asked him to appear on a float. Of course, he hadn't told anyone that he wanted to be a cat character on their float, but they should have known from the moment James had been denied that he needed to be on a float. Mother never took care of that for him, so now he was taking care of that himself. Each death had resulted in the retirement of the cat costume, either because it was damaged, or it was bad luck, or it was viewed as disrespectful. By the end of this killing spree, he hoped to have removed all of the characters from floats.

A tiny part of him knew that this was an absurd response to a childhood denial, but this was when he no longer felt his mother's love. He thought he was the center of her world but then she hadn't stood up for him, hadn't loved him enough for him to appear on the float. He must admit to himself he felt a little more loved with each float death. At times, he could even picture in his mind, his mother smiling down at him when he finished eliminating another cat character. He liked to think that she thought that being a cat character wasn't good enough for him, and if it wasn't good enough for him, it also wasn't suitable for volunteers.

With the next death in front of him, he focused on studying the promenade to see where the parade would go. As he did with most of his kills, he obtained a list of the parade entries, and there were three floats he could choose from. He briefly debated taking on all the floats, but his actions would not go undetected. He would just have to come back in future years and take care of the other two floats. He kept a list of parades to return to in the future as he had more cat characters that he needed to eliminate.

The Israeli Police were smart, and so he needed to be more careful than usual with his kill. This time he got hold of a water bottle that was the exact kind that would be placed on the float to keep the float riders hydrated during the parade. The costumed characters needed more water than average as they sweat inside the suits. They were encouraged to drink more at the start of the parade as the head part of a costume often prevented drinking during the parade. That was perfect for his plan.

He'd brought with him cyanide, and he planned to mix it into the water bottle. He could inject it near the neck of the bottle with a tiny needle, and the bottle would not look like it had been tampered with. It was odorless and tasteless, and the cat character should be dead by the end of the parade. Of course, if someone knew what was in the bottle, there were antidotes, but they never would figure that out in time. He brought several bottles with him in hopes of switching back to a regular bottle and taking the bottle with poison in it, just to remove any evidence. He watched videos that people had uploaded the previous year of the parade so he would understand what to expect in terms of crowds and police presence. He really did a lot of research on each parade to know what to expect.

He also had taken lessons from magicians in Las Vegas and Los Angeles as he often needed to move his hands in a way that people didn't notice. That training and years of video practice made him comfortable that he wouldn't be caught even if someone was filming the parade. No one would see his hands moving.

It was time to head for a historical site. James had done all the prep work he could think of, and now it was time to play tourist.

He rubbed his hands together as he walked toward the sherut that would take him to the Western Wall. While it was some distance away in Jerusalem, about an hour's drive, he had a note he wanted to leave in the Western Wall. It was a full confession of the people he'd killed. You were supposed to leave small notes of prayer, so there was no way he could list all of the parades in which he killed a cat character as there wasn't room for all the cities. Instead, his note said, 'tomorrow marks the date of my 200th kill'. May God have mercy on all the dead cats.' He knew the Western Wall's notes were emptied twice a year and buried in Jewish tradition. Furthermore, his letter wouldn't be read before it was destroyed. Even if someone did read it, they would think he was talking about domestic cats, and not parade route volunteers.

He arrived at the Wall and found a place to insert his note. He put it up fairly high in a snug place, so the wind wouldn't blow it out of the wall for all to see. Then he looked around to watch people's behavior in this remote place.

When he was done at the Wall, he started walking toward the Mount of Olives. It was five miles away, and he would catch another sherut to take him the short distance. It was a strange place with death and religion everywhere. There were Jewish and Catholic cemeteries and houses of worship. There was even a shrine to the Virgin Mary, who was purported to be buried there. James couldn't recall reading the Bible, but he had vague memories of his parents taking him to church as a child.

He was a man of death, and here he stood amid vast cemeteries and famous dead people, and he was unmoved by all of it he realized. He didn't care about the dead, or religion, or the struggles of the people buried here. Note to self, don't bother visiting places like this in the future as they completely underwhelmed him.

CHAPTER 32

Saturday arrived, and it was an exciting day for the city of Tel Aviv's children. They lined the streets every year to watch the magical parade with dreams of one day being in the parade themselves. It also meant the start of summer. There were carefree months ahead of them before they returned to school. Parents arrived early for a front-row spot at the street barricades. Some of the children came dressed in a costume of their own. The street was filled with little princesses and superheroes. The weather looked to be perfect—no rain, but not yet blazing heat. A heatwave was coming, but not today. Nothing stood in the way of the marvelous parade.

Detective Natalie Severino and Special Agent Leticia Ortiz stood next to Chief Inspector David Peretz. He was in charge of today's operation, and it felt like the entire Israeli Police Force was watching and listening through earbuds. It was a different kind of operation than usually garnered attention. He was not taking down a drug lord, an anti-Semitic terrorist, or a suicide bomber. Instead, he was taking down a man that the world wanted to stop. Someone who was a terrorist in his own right, but with a very different cause. What kind of killer focused on some-

189

thing so benign as a cat character? The dude was very mentally ill. For the length of time the murders had been happening, it had to be something from his childhood that was propelling the man to execute all these killings.

They could see Chief Inspector Peretz had the requisite officers near the parade route in what was likely their usual formation. Still, they knew he also had an additional fifty officers in a variety of jobs and posts. The officers on the parade route and on a few of the floats were in a variety of clothes that were anything but their typical uniform. There were even officers in costume. Each officer in disguise had a blue circle attached up the upper right shoulder so he or she could be readily identified without the usual badge, uniform, or sidearm. The police force had created two additional floats to replace the ones they were taking over, and these new floats had no cat costumed characters. They had put their officers in their respective cat costumes with a variety of protections. Natalie assisted the Israeli police in studying many of his previous kills and tried to think through what the killer could possibly use to kill their cat character. Half of the preparations were for protecting officers. The other half of the preparations were to make sure their killer was identified and taken into custody. It was hard to say what they, Leticia and Natalie included, feared most – losing one of their own or losing this killer. Underneath all of the preparations was the worry that it was all for nought. What if the prediction of where the killer would strike next was wrong? When Natalie looked around at the resources that had been put in place for this operation, she sent a silent prayer that Damian's computer would be correct for the second time in this case.

A few blocks away, a command center was set up with television screens showing every inch on the promenade and a few streets around the city. The cameras nearest the target float in question were using artificial intelligence to match anyone to the pictures taken by the Danish Police. The images were so general of their suspect that matches were occurring about once every thirty seconds. They had to bring in additional observers just to watch all the suspects pointed out by the camera.

The parade was underway, but it would take at least thirty minutes before the two original floats in question would move as they were towards the end of the parade. This was the prime time that the killer would be near their float if he was going to strike. The Chief Inspector had a grim look on his visage as he scanned the passersby for danger. Natalie could see the lines of stress as the Inspector was starting to feel the eye strain from staring so hard at the crowd while listening so intently to the conversation in his earpiece. Then she heard it or at least thought she did. The Israeli Police had informed their officers that there were American observers for this operation and requested the police force to speak English rather than Hebrew. Still, not every officer remembered to speak in English, and some had such thick accents that Natalie wasn't sure what they were saying.

"There's someone suspicious next to the float. Let's not lose him," the voice said, going on to describe what she saw. Then she added, "I want you to keep him in sight while I go back and review the tape."

All chatter stopped over the radio stopped while they awaited her response.

"Affirmative. The male described is our suspect. He switched water bottles. He was so quick and subtle that I had to re-watch the film in slow motion to detect his movements."

The Chief Inspector said over the microphone system, "All units, take the suspect into custody," repeating the description given him.

"Sir, this is Constable Katz, the suspect has changed clothing, and is now wearing tan colored pants, a green jacket, and a dark blue hat," stated the breathless man in a quiet voice.

"Command center confirm suspect's appearance change," commanded Peretz.

Again there was silence as he was watched on the monitors. "Confirmed."

The Chief Inspector muttered a curse word and wondered how many clothing changes the guy could affect while on the run.

They heard Peretz issue instructions, "Let's give Constable Katz backup. Who is closest to him? We need to hold our perimeter and get that bottle of water bagged and let's find out what's in it. Is it sealed? Oh, and close the borders, airports, trains, and port. Let's make sure he doesn't get out of this country."

There was a buzz of conversation as two other constables joined Katz in hurrying after a man who was slick, moving in and out of crowds, seemingly changing his clothes while walking fast, with a magician's training for the game of now you see him, now you don't.

Natalie and Leticia looked at each other, knowing they were so close, but yet so far from having their killer in custody. Natalie held up two fingers crossed together in luck, and Leticia saluted her with her own fingers crossed.

They heard Peretz ask, "Status report. Is the suspect in custody?"

"Sorry, Sir, we lost him in the crowd," came back Katz's reply.

The two women let their breath out, disappointed they were not going to get their criminal.

Then they heard from the Command Center, "Suspect is traveling towards Frishman Street. There are a lot of side streets and alleyways to lose the police in. Constable Cohen, you're the closest. Move it."

Natalie heard a long announcement in Hebrew by Paretz, who then turned off his microphone and said, "I asked the officers to hurry, but be careful. We Israelis are used to incoming fire, and seeing a bunch of police officers run would cause panic on the streets. This will cause us to lose our suspect and potentially harm families here to watch the parade."

Natalie nodded. Israel had a very different population than the

United States. Every home and business incorporated a bomb shelter. People were used to hurrying into a shelter, and with people five to seven deep at the barricades, someone could get hurt in the panic.

"I've lost the suspect," said the command center.

They heard a winded response from Constable Cohen, "I still have him in sight."

Natalie heard Peretz say, "Constable Cohen, turn on your live body camera, maybe we can see the suspect on your camera."

Then Natalie heard from the command center, "We see the suspect. Look at that, he's changing clothing again. He's slapped on a wig with a yarmulke and pulled additional clothing off. Now he's in dark pants and a brown shirt."

Natalie and Leticia were looking at the tablet that featured the live feed from Constable Cohen's body camera. It was bouncing as the officer moved quickly down the street.

Then their suspect disappeared from view.

"What the heck!" Leticia exclaimed.

Peretz said to them, "There are small side alcoves and parking ramps off that street. I'm sure that's where he disappeared to, but there aren't full streets that he can escape from. He's cornered, we just need to find him."

"Are you sure?" Natalie asked, concerned that they were so close yet so far away.

"Yes, I was raised on that street and know where there are possible places to hide as I have years of playing hide and seek. I just need to get a few more officers there."

"Can you direct us to that street?" Leticia asked.

"I can, but you have no authority and no gun in this country, Agent Ortiz."

"Actually, I've never shot someone in my own country. It's a myth that we are shooting people all the time, and besides, I left my gun back in the states."

With her assurances, he had another officer take the two

Americans to Frishman Street. They continued to monitor the conversation while they hustled over to the street in question, understanding about half of what they heard between police codes, accents, and the occasional Hebrew word.

They arrived at the base of the street and assessed the block as much as they could in a foreign country. There were Israeli officers carrying out different tasks. Some had stopped traffic, others appeared to be searching for the suspect.

"Shall we clear the street?" Leticia asked Natalie.

"Yes, what do we have to lose? I know that the Israelis officers are doing so too, but maybe we'll see something they don't."

The two approached every doorway, every alcove looking for a man based on the last description of clothing. They were happy to find building doors locked as well as parking gates. The police had stopped vehicle traffic in the street, so they took turns approaching doorways, with one of them staying in the middle of the road in case any man exited any building. Leticia was looking intently around the street, anxious as they were so close to capturing the killer. Still, she looked at the space he might be hiding in up and down the road, and she wondered if he could get away by going to the building roof and make it to another street.

Plainclothes officers were filling the block, but still no suspect in sight. Natalie glanced over as Leticia approached and said, "There, a man just peered over the edge of the apartment building."

Leticia turned and got a glimpse of the man as he moved away from the edge. She hit the talk button on the transmitter they gave her.

"Special Agent Leticia Ortiz of the FBI. I just saw a man lean over the top of one of the buildings on Frishman Street, can you get someone here to get on the roof? The building address is Thirteen A."

There was conversation back and forth, which the two Americans had trouble following.

"This is Peretz, we have a helicopter with an ETA of one minute to your location. What is the street address again?"

"Thirteen A, it's a white five-story building," Leticia said, then looking around, added, "I guess all the buildings are white here in Tel Aviv."

"Yes, Special Agent, Tel Aviv's nickname is the white city as most of our buildings are white."

"Whoops. Is there someone that can let us into the building so we can reach the roof?" Natalie asked.

"We had a special tactics team on standby for the parade, they have an ETA of two minutes to your street. You may begin to hear the approach of the helicopter," Peretz said.

"Yes, I can, but we have a killer in one of your buildings, and I want to enter it now!" Leticia said, trying to get someone to let them in the building where they briefly saw the man of the roof. What if they were wrong? Perhaps he was hiding somewhere else.

Natalie walked over the doorway of the building in question and pushed hard on the door. Then she waved Leticia over to follow her inside. They hadn't got to that doorway yet and assumed it was locked like all the others, but instead, the two women hustled up the five flights of stairs looking for the roof access door.

They were both breathing heavily by the time they reached the top. Natalie had grabbed a tree branch on the way into the building, and now that stick of wood was the only weapon that they had. They burst through the door that was marked 'exit', and some words that they couldn't read. They found themselves on a gravel roof with a helicopter not far away. It was whipping their hair around as well as some of the gravel on the roof. Natalie looked for a man, but no one was on the roof.

They heard over their earbuds, "Ortiz and Severino, are you on the roof of the building in question?"

"Yes," they both replied.

"Your suspect has jumped over to another roof. Please return to the street," they heard displeasure in Peretz's voice.

Natalie looked at Leticia and said, "We've come this far, let's go find him, although I'm not jumping from one roof to the next."

Leticia nodded, and instead of returning to the doorway to stairs inside, they walked over to the edge of the building to see where the man had gone. They saw him disappear into the other building's stairwell.

The two women eyed the drop to the next building that was connected to the one they were standing on and decided it was too big a drop.

Leticia looked at Natalie and said, "Let's run down the stairs and around this block to that building."

Natalie nodded, and they took the stairs at the fastest speed they could manage, hoping to find their killer in the next block.

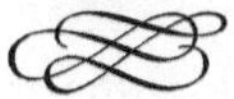

James was anxious and out of breath. The cops were on to him. If only he hadn't tried to pit himself against the Israeli Police force. How did they know he was there? Had they seen him switch bottles? Maybe the cat character was dead by now. Possibly his mission was accomplished; now, he just needed to get out of Israel. He heard the helicopter overhead and thought back to all the cameras in this city. Why hadn't he stayed out of Israel?

He would get away and never come back. It was simply too dangerous. It was a good thing he saw the sites he did on this visit as he would never again cross into Israel. While he was running down the stairs, he made his last appearance change. He started checking all the doors that he passed. If all else failed, he might find a closet to hide in or maybe a car in one of the parking lots. He found one of the apartment doors open, and so he stepped in, thinking there might be something in it that would be useful to his escape. He ran into the bedroom looking for clothes, but only a woman lived here. He pulled the woman's clothing out, but it wouldn't fit him. He dumped the clothes he'd taken off along the route under her bed, found a backpack, and quickly put his inside hers. Best of all, he found a wig in the closet. He put it on tying it with a hairband. He still looked like a guy, but with drastically different hair. Now he needed to get out of this apartment before she came back. He left money on a dresser in payment for what he borrowed and walked out to the apartment's balcony to see if he had an escape route.

James heard the front door open and decided now was the time to shimmy down a drainpipe to street level. He hoped he could make it to the end of the street and then to the public bus. He just needed to get out of the neighborhood.

Moments after landing on the sidewalk, someone walked by him and looked at him strangely, so he said, "The elevator's not working in the building, so it's faster to just slide down that pole as long as it's not rainy out."

After he spoke, James knew he gave away his American heritage with his accent and English words, but he knew nothing of the Hebrew language.

The stranger just gave him a wide berth identifying him as a crazy person, which was fine with James.

James continued at a robust pace down the street. He thought he had about one-hundred yards to go to reach the bus. He could hear the helicopter overhead and saw the bus coming just as he was crossing the street. He ran for it and hopped aboard just as it was about to pull away from the curb. He threw money in the ticket machine and sat down for the ride, which was, fortunately, heading in the direction of the port where his boat was docked.

He took his cell phone out and pondered where to exit the bus and catch some other means of transportation to the port. He worked out his route and relaxed slightly, though the wig was itchy. He would not feel relief until he reached the port and pulled away from the shores of Israel. Thankfully, he had gassed up the yacht that morning. Once he made it out of the Tel Aviv city center, he relaxed further. Every step away from that apartment building was a good thing.

Finally, he exited the bus in a neighborhood with a variety of stores, which made it easier for him to get lost in the crowd and catch a sherut to the port. He thought about the port manager and how he needed to change his appearance to something the port manager would recognize. He would have to dump the wig and buy some clothes like those he wore this morning. With the five layers, he'd pulled off while escaping the police, he probably looked a good thirty to forty pounds lighter than he had when he left his boat earlier in the day. He asked the sherut driver to wait for him while he went into a department store to bulk up on his purchases.

They arrived at the port, and James headed into a restroom to adjust his appearance. He thought he looked reasonably close to the way he'd looked that morning. So he approached the boat owner's entrance and walked through it to his boat. He started the motors and cast the lines off, preparing to leave. He began motoring out of the port and was almost clear of the sea wall. He heard an alarm sound but didn't know what that meant, and he applied maximum power to head toward Cyprus.

He pulled a beer out of the refrigerator and drank deeply as his getaway had made him thirsty. Israel's territorial waters ended at the twelve-mile mark. In thirty minutes, he would be clear and safe. Once in Cyprus, he'd fly home and skip the next kill he had scheduled. He needed to rest after nearly being caught by the Israelis. Also, once he got to his destination, he'd check the news to see if he was successful in eliminating the cat character. He had about a nine-hour boat ride in front of him, but at least he was a free man rather than sitting in an Israeli jail.

It was Monday morning, and Damian's company was back at their Richmond warehouse location. He'd notified everyone that they had been identified by the BlueSilver investigators. Still, no one felt the need for additional security. Damian walked in, carrying a container that he intended to leave in one of the company cabinets. It would be out of the vision of any visitors to their lab, but available anytime his employees needed it. The container was filled with water guns loaded with pepper juice, a bag of balloons and a dye solution to 'stain' any intruders, and a piece of cloth that reflected light in such a way as to make the wearer less visible to others. Everyone knew how to use the supplies.

They all returned to their day jobs, knowing that Damian kept an eye on the company and would alert them if things were about to get dangerous. Hermione and Jacob were continuing to write code to make their app look pretty and be slick. Jordan had weeks of programming in front of him. Viramic was happily functioning across the bay.

Damian received a call from Natalie and was curious as to how her cold case was going. Since he hadn't heard on the news that they had caught their man, he had to assume his prediction of Tel Aviv was wrong. Oh well, one of two predictions was better than none.

"Hi, so my projection of Israel was wrong?"

"No, it was correct. The killer got away. Leticia, the Israeli cops, and I chased into him into a side street. He slipped into some apartment buildings before making his escape by bus."

"Was anyone hurt?"

"No, the guy is a magician with his hands, but they still caught him substituting water bottles on the float. The bottle he placed there had cyanide in it and would have killed its intended target by the end of the parade."

"Did you get any evidence? Any pictures or fingerprints or DNA?"

"We did. We got a few photographs. We also located an apartment that he went through in his dash away from the police. The woman who owns the apartment found her wig and backpack missing, and money left behind to presumably pay for those losses. She called the police to report the burglary as the money he left behind didn't begin to cover the wig's cost. Police asked if they could search her apartment further, and she agreed. They found the various outfits he taken off in his escape tucked under her bed. We actually saw on a live camera that he would pull off a pair of pants while walking down the street. They apparently had Velcro holding them together. So the police found DNA and fingerprints that they are running now. They closed the trains, roads, airports, and seaports, but he must have slipped away before the alarm went out. There was a port north of Tel Aviv that was slow to close, and a boat left just as the alarm was sounding."

"So, do you need another prediction of where he'll strike next?"

"I think all bets are off. He knew he was being chased, which had to be a first for him. He may choose to lay low for a while. By the way, the port people identified him as an American, although the passport was a fake. He's another blight on America's record of raising serial killers."

"Well, if you have any fingerprints or DNA that you want me to run, just give me a call."

"Actually, that's is why I'm calling. Leticia was able to convince them to give us copies of the evidence. It's just taken a little while to come in. I think the Israelis wanted a go at the evidence before turning it over to us, but alas, they had no luck. Aren't they famous for their computer brains?"

"They are famous. They have invented some of the most popular computer programs in use today. That brilliant navigation program you use in your car every day is thanks to them."

"But, you're smarter, right?"

"Ah, no. I think you probably already had the best computer jocks take a look at the evidence. Still send it my way, and I'll see if I can do anything with it. Who knows, maybe I'll have an advantage as he's an American."

"That's what I'm hoping. Don't you have a source that's tied into airport security, and with this guy flying all over the world, he's got to be in your database."

"Maybe, but he also seems like he's the king of disguises. Send me everything, and I'll see what I can do with it."

The two of them spoke a while longer then Damian saw the email arrive with some large attachments.

After he ended the call, he went to work, trying to get an identity of Natalie's serial killer. He set his computer to search with the information she sent him and went back to work on BlueSilver's CEO Fred Rodgers, trying to determine if he was a threat or not. He'd also rigged another program to notify him if someone matching the visage of any of the private investigators employed by Consolidated Security Systems approached the building.

Damian was looking for evidence that Mr. Rodgers might hire someone to damage this warehouse. Still, he gave up as he was convinced that whatever Fred was going to do, he would buy

Bitcoin and make the arrangements on the dark web. If Damian tried to search that part of the internet, he would be unsuccessful.

He sighed and decided to check on Jordan to see how he was doing with the app aimed at helping law enforcement. It was a big undertaking, and he wasn't sure if Jordan would complete it before returning to school in the fall. He frequently checked on the teen and monitored his activity online. Damian didn't trust him with access to the law enforcement database. It wasn't personal, rather he knew teenagers to be impulsive and curious. He let Jordan know that he was checking on him, to make sure the kid kept on the straight and narrow. He also mapped out for the teen how he wanted the app designed. If Damian hadn't had this company, he might have spent months doing the coding himself on his island, but things were different now. In fact, when he looked back on his life, he should have designed this app years ago, but sometimes you had to be in the right place in your life to think of these creations.

"Jordan, how is it going? Do you need help with anything?"

Jordan was excited about his work and the computer mentor that Damian Green was. When he introduced him to the visiting officers a week ago, it had put a face on who his app would help and how they needed such technology. Jordan would have worked night and day to get this done, but he hadn't figured out how to hack into the various law enforcement platforms like Damian had. So his work stopped each night when he went home. He was motivated not to play online games late into the evening as he wanted to get up early to get to work. His parents had even noticed his behavior change and commented, to his embarrassment.

"I could get this done faster if you would let me work late on it."

"Jordan, we've been over this before. First, your parents would be unhappy. Second, the State of California Labor Department would sue me for breaking child labor laws; third, you're young, impulsive, and open to peer pressure. I like having you where I can monitor what you're up to so you don't stray from the straight and narrow. Besides, don't you need my help when you've backed yourself into a coding corner?"

Jordan sighed, and then they all ducked to the ground as they heard a loud rumble followed by breaking glass.

CHAPTER 35

Damian yelled, "Everyone get down!" even though his voice was drowned out by the noise of breaking glass and a part of the building falling away.

He was on his belly and pulled his cell phone off his belt, dialing 9-1-1.

"What is your emergency?" came the operator.

"There's just been an explosion at my building."

"Are there injuries? What is your address?"

Damian reeled off his address and then replied, "There's so much smoke and dust, I can't tell if there are injuries."

"Police and fire have been dispatched to your location. Please stay on the line, Sir."

"Sorry, I've got to check on my people," Damian said, ending the phone call. Help was on its way, and that was all that mattered.

Damian stood up and checked on Jordan first as he had been closest to him.

"Jordan, are you okay?"

He peered out from under a desk with white drywall dust coloring his hair.

"I'm fine. I'll help you check the others."

Damian went looking for Hermione and Jacob next. He could hear the wail of approaching sirens. The dust was settling somewhat, and he could see the far side of the warehouse wall was missing, He could view the blue sky. He pulled his shirt up over his face to avoid inhaling the dusty air.

Damian made his way toward where the teenagers had been working, and he was happy to see they seemed unharmed although dirty.

"Hermione, Jacob, are you guys okay?"

"We're fine. In fact, we all seem fine except Haley, who isn't moving around," Hermione said, pointing to the ground about ten feet in front of them.

Damian rushed over to Haley, as did the others. Damian debated turning her over, but not knowing her injuries, he decided to wait for the paramedics.

"Should we move her?" asked Hermione. She put her hands on Haley as if ready to assist with turning her over.

Damian shook his head and said, "We don't know what her injuries are. If she injured her neck in the fall, then it needs to be immobilized before she's moved.

"I'm fine," came a grunt. "Something hit me in the head. I'll turn myself over."

Haley seemed to be waiting for something, then she rolled over, and everyone gasped. She had blood running down her face from a cut somewhere near her hairline. She put a dusty hand up to the blood, but Hermione grasped it before Haley reached her target.

"Haley, don't touch your face. Our hands are covered in dust, and I can see an open cut near your hairline, and you don't want to get dust in it."

"Okay," she mumbled.

Damian stood up and walked over toward the opening in the side of the building. He could see what remained of a car that had been blown to kingdom come. He looked around inside the warehouse, and the far walls seemed to be stable. He walked over to unlock the entrance doors to his business. He propped it open for whatever rescue group was coming up the stairs. He saw a police officer and fire person approaching.

"Hi. I'm Damian Green, I called you for an explosion."

"Did you have an accident here?" asked the officer, looking around.

"No, this is a crime scene," and he waved the officer over to the hole in his building. He didn't walk over to the edge as he was worried about structural damage, but he wanted to point out to the cop what was left of the mangled car.

"Are you saying that a car explosion caused this damage?"

"Well, it didn't come from anything inside this building. Are paramedics on the way? I have an injured employee."

"Yes, Sir. We were just clearing the scene before we sent them up. Can you evacuate all of your employees from the building while we get some resources here to check for further explosives or structural damage?" when he finished his sentence, he radioed for the paramedics to come up.

Damian asked his employees to exit the building and wait in Pete's restaurant if it was undamaged. He hoped the restaurant was undamaged as it was on nearly the opposite side of the building as the car bomb, and with the crime scene, it wouldn't be opening today. He returned to Haley's side and asked, "How are you feeling?"

"Better now that help is here, but I've already got a headache."

"Paramedics will be here in a few seconds."

"Seconds?"

"Yes, they're downstairs waiting to hear from the cops that they are safe to enter. In case we had any more bombs here."

Her eyes were closed in pain, and Haley gave him a faint grin.

"They wouldn't ask such a stupid question if they had seen the number of times I've crashed the drones in this space."

Damian was about to reply, but true to his word, the paramedics set heavy utility boxes down next to Haley and began asking her questions. He stepped away from her and looked around at the computers. With a bunch of strangers about to enter his premises, he wanted to make sure the computers were secure – both in terms of pass-codes and outright theft. He would need to get someone here with plywood to block the hole until the building could be repaired. He took a moment to call Ariana and let her know that Hermione and the others were all safe except for Haley, who didn't appear to have terrible injuries. He got off the phone quickly with her, then called Trevor Severino, Haley's husband, and Natalie's son.

At Trevor's request, he called him back on a video call so he could see Haley for himself. She was sitting up, while the paramedics treated her head wound. They had decided she would go to the hospital to have someone stitch up the wound and check for a concussion. Trevor was relieved to see her talking.

"I'm leaving the office now. What hospital are they taking her to? I'll meet her there."

"Kaiser, Richmond. I would send someone to stay with her, so she's not alone until you arrive, but we are all witnesses, and so we have to stay here."

"No problem. Thank you for calling and arranging the video call. I can see she's hurt, but at least now I won't drive like a desperate maniac. Will you call Mom and explain?"

"Yes. Drive safe."

He ended that call, then reached Natalie.

"Hey Natalie, I'm calling to let you know there's been an explosion here at my warehouse, and Haley's been hurt. Trevor is on his way. The paramedics are taking her to Kaiser to have a head wound stitched up and check Haley for a concussion."

There was a pause, and Damian was sure she was alternating between being a mom and being a cop.

Finally, she asked, "Are the police there?"

"Yes."

"What kind of explosion? Was there a bomb?"

"The police and fire are here investigating. Judging by a mangled car outside, it was a bomb. I can see daylight through the far side of the building."

"Was anyone else hurt?"

"No. We're all covered in drywall dust, but otherwise we're good. I'll send you a picture of Haley, so you know she's going to be okay.

"Damian, thanks for calling. My husband and I are on the way."

He made one more call to Jordan's parents in case they were watching the news, but ended up leaving a voicemail that he was safe.

Once the calls were out of the way, Haley on her way to the hospital, and the computers shut down, he joined his employees at Pete's Restaurant to wait out a conversation they would all be having with the cops.

It was approaching the lunch hour, and Pete had given his staff the day off, knowing his restaurant wouldn't be opening. Damian joined his team, and Pete placed a wheat beer in front of him, which he drank greedily as he felt like his throat was full of plaster dust.

"What the latest news?" Hermione asked.

"Haley is at the hospital getting her head sewn up and an x-ray to determine if she has a concussion. Trevor and Natalie are on their way here to be with her. There wasn't fire inside the building, and it appears that none of our equipment has been damaged. Inspectors are looking at the far end of the warehouse to determine if it is structurally sound. Depending on what the engineers say, we'll either move to a new location while this place gets rebuilt if there's structural damage. Or I'll be hiring a cleaning service to get the dust out of there, patch up the wall and install a new window at that end. We needed more natural light, but this wasn't the way I planned on it happening. Pete, I think that you'll be able to open tomorrow as this place wasn't touched."

"Who bombed us?" asked Jacob.

"Was it BlueSilver?" asked Hermione.

"Kiddo, I don't know. I didn't have a warning that Mr. Rodgers might go there, but you can bet that I'm going to research him once I get home tonight. That is unless the cops come up with anything else."

"Are you going to tell the police about him?" asked Angus.

"I don't know. We don't have any direct threats from Mr. Rodgers. I suppose I'll mention the private investigators he hired, and let them take it from there."

"Don't you have cameras on this building?" Lily asked.

Damian slapped his forehead and said, "Of course I do. I don't know why I didn't think of looking there."

He opened the laptop he carried with him and hit several keys. Then he brought up the building security and turned the laptop around so they could all watch. There was silence as everyone watched the screen. They saw the car in question pull into their parking lot then drive over to the grassy area at the end near where the car had exploded. The vehicle had no license plates, and the vehicle identification number had probably been blown to bits. The driver got out, and it appeared to be a man. He continued to walk along the side of the building toward the marina when the building cameras lost sight of him.

Seconds later, they all leaned back as they saw the car explode on the laptop. Apparently, the flying debris damaged Damian's security cameras as the screen when dark shortly after that.

"Thank goodness I wasn't leaning against that wall when the explosion occurred. I often lean there out of the way of Haley's drones." Angus said.

"I think our bomb person was dumb and we had luck on our side," Chris said, and the others nodded.

"Or they didn't know our interior configuration, and just

assumed we inhabited the first floor on this side of the building," Angus said.

Damian felt his watch buzz with a text. He viewed it and said, "Haley's fine. No concussion, and she's been stitched up."

A cheer went up over that, just as the door opened and the police and fire people stepped in. They had raised brows at the group cheering, so Damian said, "We just got word that Haley doesn't have any other injuries than that gash."

They smiled at that and said, "That's good news. Obviously, this is a crime scene, and so we need to interview each of you separately for our report," the cop said. Then looking at the teenagers, he asked, "How old are each of you?"

Damian sighed and said, "Jacob is fifteen, and Hermione and Jordan are sixteen. Lily is Jacob's guardian, and I'm Hermione's guardian. If you want to take a statement from Jordan, you'll have to get his parents here. I will say that he and I were standing next to each other at the time of the explosion, so you may not need a statement from him. I'd also like to show you the explosion on camera."

"Actually, if you have video of the bomb detonating, I'll skip interviewing everyone under eighteen."

Damian pulled it up, and he and his crew got out of the way as the police and fire personnel watched the explosion several times.

After they finished, Damian sent them both a copy of the footage.

"This is interesting. Do you have any other camera angles on the suspect?"

"I'm afraid not. Perhaps you have cameras for the streets of Richmond or the marina, as that looked like the direction the suspect was walking."

"I'll inquire. Who wants you or your company dead? What's the motive here? What kind of business is your company? Are you the company that the FBI and SJPD visited about two to three weeks ago?"

Good, thought Damian. They had a smart cop on their hands who was connecting the dots.

"Yes, this was the company they visited. We engineer products and build software. As for motive, my only guess is the CEO of the BlueSilver Company as we are building a technology that will greatly diminish his sales. He's hired a private investigator company to watch us, and perhaps they weren't too ethical to try and kill us. By the way, I'm trying to make plans for tomorrow. Will you be done with the building tonight? Can I hire a cleaning crew and get the side of the building boarded up?"

Now the fire inspector spoke, "You are fortunate that your support beams in this building are made of steel. They weren't damaged by the explosion, and once we are done tonight, you'll be able to get back in the building tomorrow."

"Let's return to your statement about the BlueSilver Company, tell me what is going on. Are you business rivals?" asked the cop.

"No. My company is designing an app for your smartphone that will allow you to block Bluetooth beacons whenever you enter a store. Currently, consumers are tracked for their shopping behavior. They may be offered coupons, and retail leaders know what consumer interest is inside a store. My app will block beacons from communicating with your phone. That will likely cause a decrease in sales of the beacons. Mr. Rodgers' entire company and revenues are based on sales of those beacons. Two private investigators followed the three teens to lunch one day listening in on their conversation. Fortunately, one of the teens took a picture, and I was able to trace the person to Consolidated Security. I could see that BlueSilver hired the company. If you would like to follow up with those investigators, their names are Shelly Monson and Michael Swatten. To be clear, Consolidated appears to be a good company. Still, if I were of Mr. Rodgers' mindset, I would have purchased the bomb-maker on the dark web with Bitcoin."

"This is really a wild story," said the cop.

"How many cars have been blown up next to a business in your career?" Damian asked.

"None." replied the cop after thinking about it.

"So, a wild story has a role in this crime scene."

"Apparently," agreed the officer.

Eventually, after more discussion, Damian and his people were free to go.

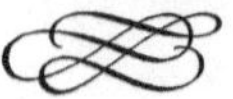

CHAPTER 36

Hermione and Damian arrived at the dock loaded down with stuff again. After some thought, Damian decided to move their offices back to Red Rock Island until Damian or the police figured out who was behind the bombing. Their boat was loaded with computers and other equipment used by the group.

"Gee whiz, I can't keep you safe. Even at work, someone wants to attack you."

"I'm just a trouble magnet. Hopefully, I'll outgrow that at some time," Hermione said.

After a short trip out to the island, they unloaded stuff and gave Ariana a call. Then they made dinner and called it an evening. Hermione's adrenaline rush from the bombing had dissipated, leaving her exhausted and ready for bed.

Damian returned to his basement lab, recalling that he had started the run on Natalie's serial killer. As it was being run in the cloud, his computer should have still been thinking even though he was distracted elsewhere.

He logged in and looked at the runs he'd asked the computer to do. He was blown away by the result. Their suspect applied for

Global Entry, the program that gives you expedited rights to get through Customs and Immigration. To get the pass for the special program, all ten fingerprints are recorded. Amazingly, he also had a Canadian passport that required his fingerprints. Damian would have thought he was a dual citizen, except he had a different name on each of them. Both passports were a match to the fingerprints. Damian looked for an address because wouldn't it be cool if they could just march in and arrest the dude. Finding one surprisingly in San Francisco, he called Natalie.

"Hi, Damian. If you're calling to check on Haley, she's doing fine. Her head is sore, and she's going to have to stay out of the sun until the incision heals, but other than that, there are no anticipated long-term problems. We convinced her to take a day off work tomorrow."

"That's great, Natalie. I was delighted to hear she didn't have a concussion. I found your serial killer, and his address is in San Francisco."

"What?!!"

"I started your run just before we were bombed today, and I forgot about it until about thirty minutes ago. I logged into my computer to see what it had done and found a fingerprint match for the prints on the clothing."

"OMG. Let me get Special Agent Ortiz on the phone, as she'll do a good job capturing this guy. Just a moment."

Damian listened to the silence of hold for a short time, and then he heard the Special Agent's crisp voice.

"Damian, you've identified our killer?"

"Yes, and his address is about four blocks from your FBI building. You could walk down the street and arrest him."

"Can you meet me at the FBI building, Damian? I have a feeling I could use your skills in an operation like this one."

"Sorry, my warehouse in Richmond was bombed today, and Hermione is asleep on my island. I can't leave her alone, nor am I going to wake up an exhausted teenager."

"You were bombed? Never mind, you can tell me that story later. Can't you find someone to stay with her?"

Damian sighed, thinking he didn't want this guy to slip away, but he couldn't leave Hermione alone.

"Hold on a moment," he said and then dialed Ariana. She answered, and he said. "I need a big favor from you. The FBI wants my help in catching a serial killer right now. I don't feel good about leaving Hermione alone here, given the bombing today. Could you drive your boat over and stay the night while I head into San Francisco?"

"There's a big story in there, but yes, I can help. Let me pack a bag and get Miguel's stuff. I'll be over in twenty minutes."

"Thanks. See you soon," he said, ending the call with Ariana and reconnecting with Leticia and Natalie.

"Okay, I have help on the way. She'll be at my home in twenty minutes, and then it will take me another twenty minutes to get across the bay. Can you have a ride for me at the marina in about forty minutes?"

"Yes. Natalie, are you coming?"

"I would except my daughter-in-law was injured in the bombing of Damian's business today. She's fine now, but I'm up in Richmond. Let me know what I can do from afar."

"Okay, Natalie, but be here around nine tomorrow as with any luck, we'll be announcing the arrest of this most wanted killer."

"Will do," and they ended the call.

Damian packed his laptop, a jacket for the cold drive, and proceeded to get his dock and speedy watercraft out and onto the bay. While waiting for Ariana's arrival, he began searching for a floor plan of the address their killer was at. He found it and had just forwarded it to Leticia when Ariana's boat rounded the cove heading for his dock. He helped her tie down her boat, kissed her, and gave Miguel a quick pat.

"I'm going to head to San Francisco, and I'll call you to tell you what's up once I navigate around the rocks."

She nodded and headed inside to his lab and upstairs to his bedroom. Miguel could smell Hermione and whimpered to be let into her bedroom, but Ariana didn't want to disturb her, so she dragged the dog upstairs to bed. She had just settled into Damian's bed when he called to tell her about his day and the job he was doing at the moment for the FBI. Ariana was excited for him as this serial killer was an awful person. He had another call come in from the FBI agent, so he cut their call short.

"Where are you?"

"I just passed Alcatraz, and the Gashouse Harbor is in view. Another ten minutes and the boat will be docked, and I'll be waiting out front on Marina Boulevard for a ride."

"Good. We need you here. Look for a large black SUV."

Damian put down the phone to navigate the harbor at night. Fortunately, he had docked in this marina before and knew the process. Right on time, he approached a black SUV parked on Marina Boulevard. It had red and blue emergency lights flashing to account for it taking up one lane of the four-lane street.

Damian approached the vehicle, and its passenger side window rolled down.

"Mr. Green?" came the voice from inside. "May I see some identification?"

Damian held out his wallet that included his driver's license, and the door locks clicked. Damian entered the vehicle and then held on as the driver flashed his lights and cut off the little traffic that was there at that time of night and sped toward the FBI building.

"I would like to arrive in one piece," Damian said. "I have a teenage daughter I'm raising."

"Not to worry, Sir, I've had extensive driver training. You'll arrive quickly and in one piece."

Moments later, Damian found he was correct as they were soon entering an underground garage of a large cement building. He had to assume he was in the right place. The driver parked the car and escorted him to an elevator and upstairs to a conference room.

It was filled with jackets stamped with FBI, San Francisco Police Department, or San Francisco Sheriff's Department clothing.

As far as he could determine, he was the only civilian in the room.

Leticia approached and said, "Thanks for coming. You can find information faster than anyone I know. Can you plug in your laptop to the projector and start sharing some information with everyone?"

"Sure, what would you like first?"

"Share the various pictures of our suspect from the Tel Aviv police and his passports. Then I'll want to go to the floor plan of his building, and a map of the surrounding buildings."

Damian did as requested, thinking he was a glorified data geek, but better that than one of the officers going in with a gun to capture this guy.

Leticia called the room to order sharing information as planned. She stood near a whiteboard, plotting the operation's steps in conjunction with the experts in the room. Surveillance of James King's building indicated he was in residence at the moment.

"Mr. Damian Green is a civilian consultant who has helped us predict where the killer would strike and therefore prevented two deaths. He has identified our suspect, something both the Israeli Police and the FBI failed to do. Just believe whatever he shows us in this room."

That was an embarrassing introduction, thought Damian.

Quickly, she had him run through the range of cases over the years, the recent murder attempts in Copenhagen and Tel Aviv, and the match of fingerprints to the Global Entry. Clearly, people were puzzled over his access as a civilian to all these government files. Still, as it was getting them what they wanted, no one was protesting.

The Special Agent worked out a plan to assault James King's penthouse. They even were putting people on the balcony of his penthouse to stop his escape or suicide by trying to depart through his balcony. FBI behaviorists' profile of their killer suggested he was narcissistic and so unlikely to commit suicide. Still, it was better to cover all their bases. Damian supplied the crime scene folks with a list of the 'weapons' he used over the years to search his apartment for them.

It was one in the morning, and law enforcement set out to take their man into custody. It was an uneventful arrest as, like every other bully, Mr. King put up no fight. As soon as he was in custody, Damian notified Special Agent Ortiz that he was returning home. He packed up his laptop, and fortunately, Leticia took a moment to find a ride for Damian back to the marina.

A short time later, he was crawling into bed with Ariana, who woke up when he entered the bedroom. Miguel had greeted him, and his collar made noise doing so.

Damian whispered, "The FBI has their man, and so I'm going to sleep."

He followed his words and was asleep within seconds. There was just too much excitement that day to stay conscious any longer.

CHAPTER 37

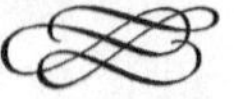

Ariana left Damian sleeping the next morning. He mentioned that the staff would be working from his place today, and so it was time to get the island ready to receive guests. She knocked on Hermione's bedroom door.

The door opened, and she could see that the teen was still in her nightclothes, she yawned and asked, "When did you get here?"

"Last night. Damian had to go help the FBI at a late hour, and he didn't want you left alone on the island given the building bombing of yesterday. Your co-workers are going to be here in an hour, so we need to get things ready. Damian is still asleep, and let us leave him that way."

Hermione nodded, "Okay, I'll be up for breakfast in fifteen minutes."

Ariana nodded and left Miguel with the teen. She went outside to the dock and pulled her pontoon forward to make room for the other boat to arrive. Then she returned upstairs to prepare breakfast for her and Hermione and feed the dog and cats. Bella and Bailey liked to spend the night hunting and sleep inside during the day. Fortunately, Damian still had some fresh fish in the refrigerator, and soon all three animals enjoyed their breakfast.

She quietly made breakfast and left extra for Damian once he woke up. She and Hermione ate while Ariana informed her about the serial killer Damian had helped catch the previous evening. Soon, they were down at the dock, welcoming the crew to work for the day. Ariana explained Damian's absence, and their need to avoid loud noises that might wake him up.

Just before lunch, he joined everyone in his lab for a briefing. He'd been awake for a while, and after showering, he watched the news conference about James King. He was pleased to see Special Agent Ortiz introduce Natalie Severino to discuss how the case started and seated behind her on stage had been relatives of the murdered victims from Morgan Hill and Evergreen Valley. It seemed that Mr. King had cracked under questioning from a specially trained FBI interviewer. He'd pushed all of James' buttons until he exploded with pride at all the work he'd done across the world going so far as to tell them where he kept his charts of parade murders. That was one smart, but monstrous dude who would be locked away from society.

During a quiet moment last night, Damian managed to extract a promise from the Agent in return for his help on the case. He wanted something done about Fred Rodgers. He was furious about the attack on his building and staff. He also had a sense that his local police might not be following up on the leads about Fred. Damian had taken a time-honored approach to bring down Fred Rodgers. He hacked into his income tax records and found lots of errors in his tax files. Specifically, he was hiding income in a fake corporation in Nevada. Damian guessed that it might be on the magnitude of fifty million dollars.

Leticia had promised that sometime this week, she would partner with the Treasury Department to serve Fred Rodgers a subpoena for his tax records under criminal investigation for tax fraud. Damian debated asking to join them in the meeting with Fred to watch. Still, he knew it was better if Fred never knew that

Damian Green was behind the two most significant threats to his life.

His company continued to meet on his island until late Friday when he received a message from Leticia. It contained a link to a business news article about Fred Rodgers, CEO of BlueSilver Company. He had been served with an arrest warrant by the U.S. Treasury Department for tax fraud. He was to be arraigned on Monday, and all of his known financial assets were frozen.

He looked up from his reading and announced, "Good news, folks. We should be safely able to return to the warehouse on Monday. The building repairs have been completed, and more importantly, Fred Rodgers, CEO of BlueSilver, has been charged with income tax evasion. If the government is successful in prosecuting him, he'll owe millions in back taxes and serve six to ten years in prison. Sometimes it's easier to prove tax evasion than connect a person to a bombing."

A cheer went up, and Damian said, "What if we take the two boats we have parked out front over to the marina bar, and we can head inside for happy hour drinks, and Shirley Temple spritzes," he said smiling at the frowning teenagers.

It had been an eventful week; he could use the camaraderie of the people inside his lab, mixed with a little alcohol, and perhaps a live sporting event to chill out. The multiple crises had come to an end, and they were all safe.

The End

ABOUT THE AUTHOR

I reside in Northern California with my rescue dog and cat. I love to travel, play sports, read, and drink wine and beer. I enjoy the diversity of the world and I'm always watching people and events for story ideas. All of my stories are generated by my imagination, I don't use AI to write books.

If you would like to sign up for my bi-weekly blog and announcement of new books, please follow this link: https://www.AlecPecheBooks.com

While you're waiting for the next story, if you would be so kind as to leave a review for this book, that would be great. I appreciate all the feedback and support. Reviews buoy my spirits and stoke the fires of creativity.

Readers that sign up for my blog receive a free prequel novelette for the Jill Quint Series.

ALSO BY ALEC PECHE

Jill Quint, MD Forensic Pathologist Series

Time's Up (prequel short story)

Vials

Chocolate Diamonds

A Breck Death

Death On A Green

A Taxing Death

Murder At The Podium

Castle Killing

Crescent City Murder

Sicilian Murder

Opus Murder

Forensic Murder

Return to the Scene of the Crime (short story)

Embers of Murder

Ashes to Murder

Mint Death

Damian Green Series

Red Rock Island

Willow Glen Heist

The Girl From Diana Park

Evergreen Valley Murder

Long Delayed Justice

Michelle Watson Series

Now You Don't See Me

Where Did She Go?

How Did She Get There?

<u>Dog Humor</u>

Eat, Play, Poop: Letters to my parents from camp

<u>New Urban Fantasy Series - Stephanie Jones</u>

The Awakening at Lake Tahoe (short story)

Witch's Medicine (2024)

www.ingramcontent.com/pod-product-compliance
Lightning Source LLC
Chambersburg PA
CBHW021136190726
48288CB00008B/2682